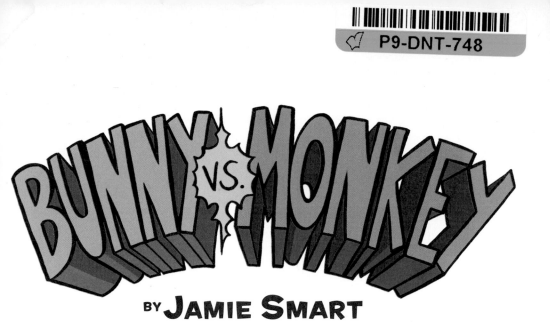

BUNNY VS. MONKEY

BY JAMIE SMART

FICKLING
d b
David Fickling Books
the PHOENIX
SCHOLASTIC

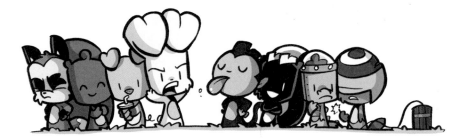

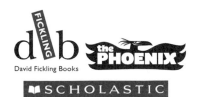

For Sarah

All rights reserved. Published by Scholastic Inc., *Publishers since 1920*, by arrangement with David Fickling Books, Oxford, England. SCHOLASTIC and associated logos are trademarks and/or registered trademarks of Scholastic Inc. DAVID FICKLING BOOKS, THE PHOENIX, and associated logos are trademarks and/or registered trademarks of David Fickling Books.

First published in the United Kingdom in 2014 as *Bunny vs Monkey: Year One* by David Fickling Books, 31 Beaumont Street, Oxford OX1 2NP. www.davidficklingbooks.com

Library of Congress Control Number Available

ISBN 978-0-545-86184-7

10 9 8 7 6 5 4 3 2 1   16 17 18 19 20

Printed in the U.S.A.   40
First edition, February 2016

MONKEY-TOPIA

THE CONTENTS

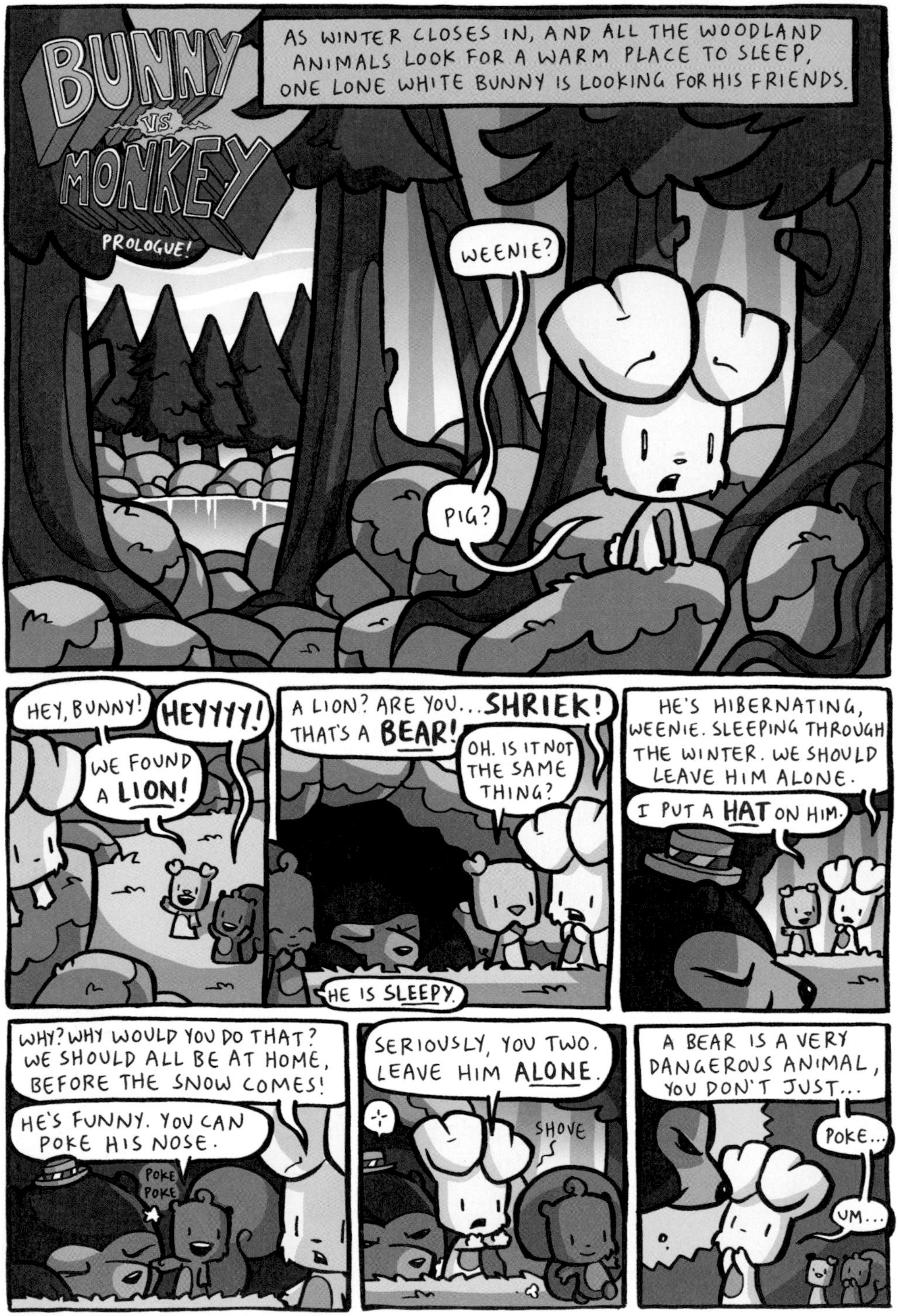

BUNNY VS MONKEY
PROLOGUE!
AS WINTER CLOSES IN, AND ALL THE WOODLAND ANIMALS LOOK FOR A WARM PLACE TO SLEEP, ONE LONE WHITE BUNNY IS LOOKING FOR HIS FRIENDS.
WEENIE?
PIG?
HEY, BUNNY!
HEYYYY!
WE FOUND A LION!
A LION? ARE YOU... SHRIEK! THAT'S A BEAR!
OH. IS IT NOT THE SAME THING?
HE IS SLEEPY.
HE'S HIBERNATING, WEENIE. SLEEPING THROUGH THE WINTER. WE SHOULD LEAVE HIM ALONE.
I PUT A HAT ON HIM.
WHY? WHY WOULD YOU DO THAT? WE SHOULD ALL BE AT HOME, BEFORE THE SNOW COMES!
HE'S FUNNY. YOU CAN POKE HIS NOSE.
POKE POKE
SERIOUSLY, YOU TWO. LEAVE HIM ALONE.
SHOVE
A BEAR IS A VERY DANGEROUS ANIMAL, YOU DON'T JUST...
POKE...
UM...

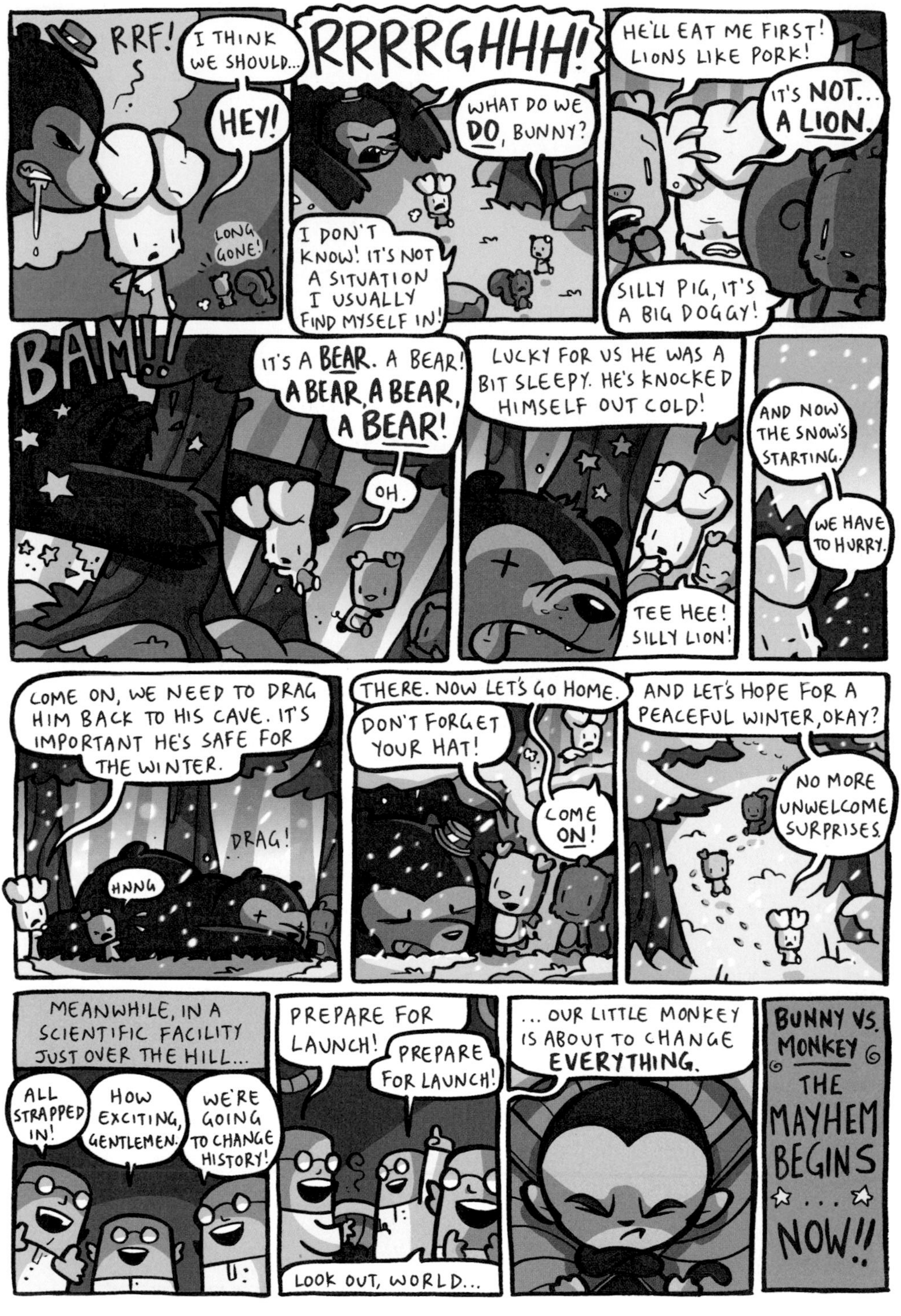
RRF!
I THINK WE SHOULD...
HEY!
LONG GONE!
RRRRGHHH!
WHAT DO WE DO, BUNNY?
I DON'T KNOW! IT'S NOT A SITUATION I USUALLY FIND MYSELF IN!
HE'LL EAT ME FIRST! LIONS LIKE PORK!
IT'S NOT... A LION.
SILLY PIG, IT'S A BIG DOGGY!
BAM!!
IT'S A BEAR. A BEAR! A BEAR, A BEAR, A BEAR!
OH.
LUCKY FOR US HE WAS A BIT SLEEPY. HE'S KNOCKED HIMSELF OUT COLD!
TEE HEE! SILLY LION!
AND NOW THE SNOW'S STARTING.
WE HAVE TO HURRY.
COME ON, WE NEED TO DRAG HIM BACK TO HIS CAVE. IT'S IMPORTANT HE'S SAFE FOR THE WINTER.
DRAG!
HNNG
THERE. NOW LET'S GO HOME.
DON'T FORGET YOUR HAT!
COME ON!
AND LET'S HOPE FOR A PEACEFUL WINTER, OKAY?
NO MORE UNWELCOME SURPRISES.
MEANWHILE, IN A SCIENTIFIC FACILITY JUST OVER THE HILL...
ALL STRAPPED IN!
HOW EXCITING, GENTLEMEN.
WE'RE GOING TO CHANGE HISTORY!
PREPARE FOR LAUNCH!
PREPARE FOR LAUNCH!
LOOK OUT, WORLD...
... OUR LITTLE MONKEY IS ABOUT TO CHANGE EVERYTHING.
BUNNY VS. MONKEY
THE MAYHEM BEGINS ... NOW!!

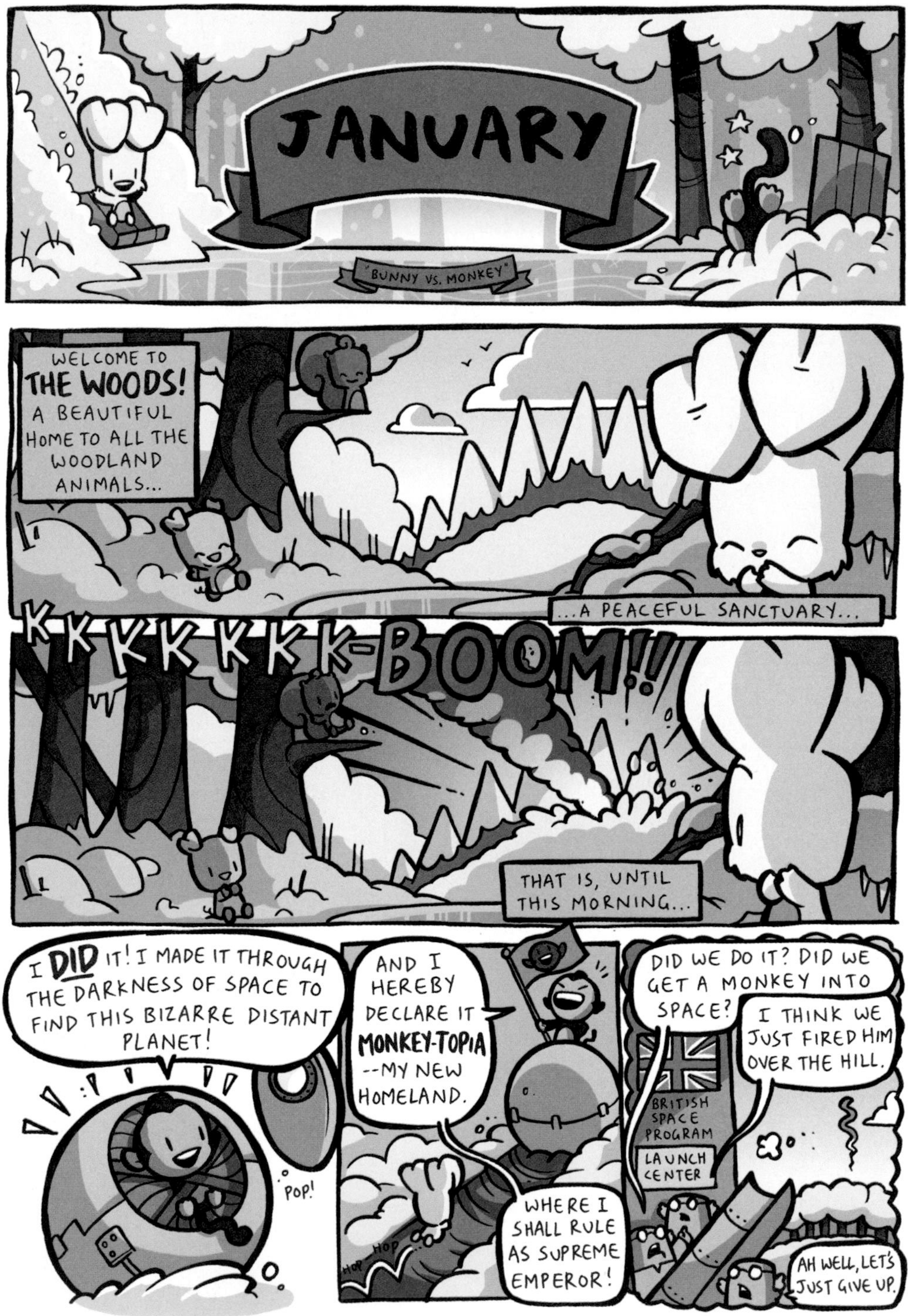

JANUARY
"BUNNY VS. MONKEY"
WELCOME TO THE WOODS! A BEAUTIFUL HOME TO ALL THE WOODLAND ANIMALS...
...A PEACEFUL SANCTUARY...
KKKKKKK-BOOM!!!
THAT IS, UNTIL THIS MORNING...
I DID IT! I MADE IT THROUGH THE DARKNESS OF SPACE TO FIND THIS BIZARRE DISTANT PLANET!
POP!
AND I HEREBY DECLARE IT MONKEY-TOPIA --MY NEW HOMELAND.
HOP HOP
WHERE I SHALL RULE AS SUPREME EMPEROR!
DID WE DO IT? DID WE GET A MONKEY INTO SPACE?
I THINK WE JUST FIRED HIM OVER THE HILL.
BRITISH SPACE PROGRAM
LAUNCH CENTER
AH WELL, LET'S JUST GIVE UP.

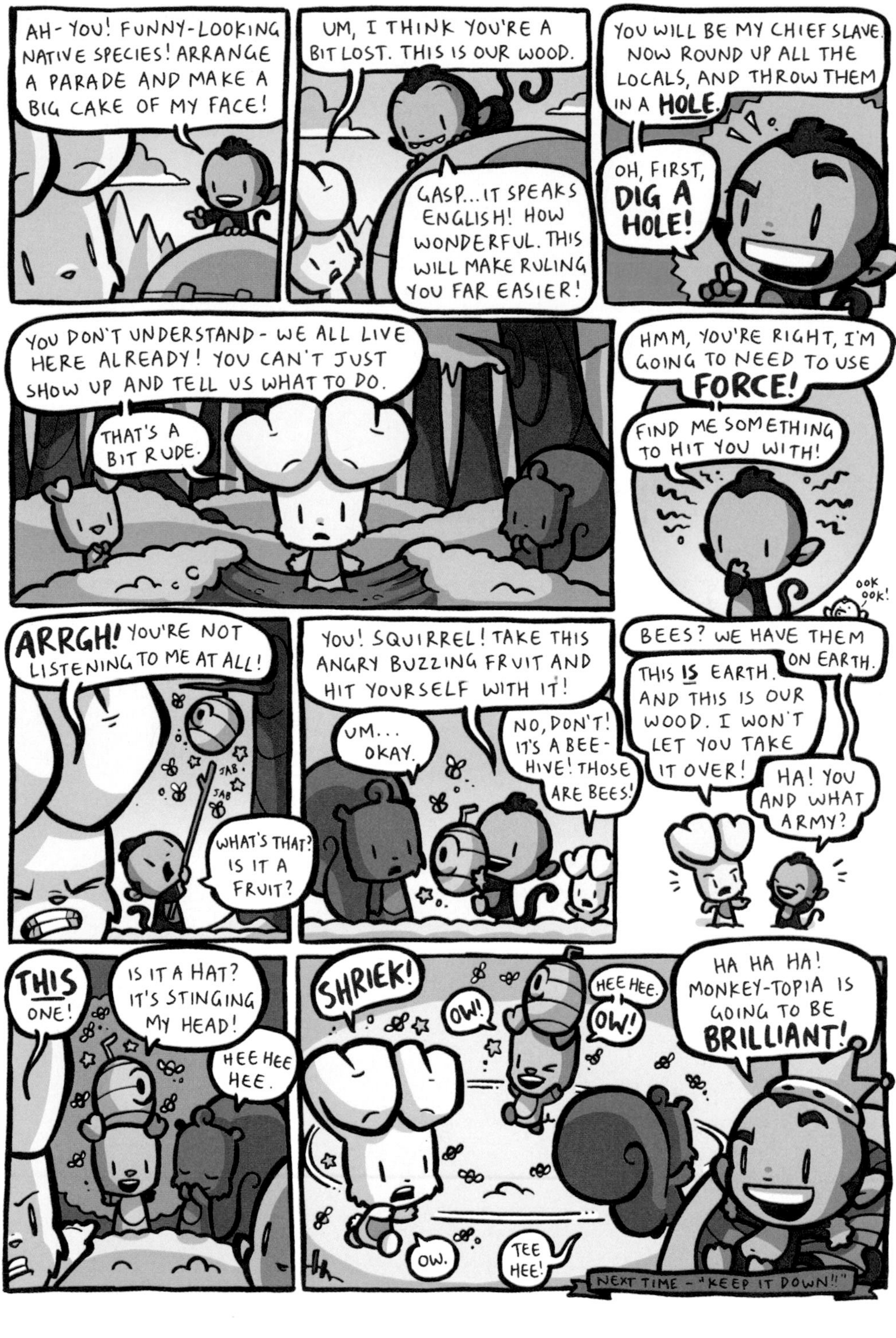
AH- YOU! FUNNY-LOOKING NATIVE SPECIES! ARRANGE A PARADE AND MAKE A BIG CAKE OF MY FACE!
UM, I THINK YOU'RE A BIT LOST. THIS IS OUR WOOD.
GASP... IT SPEAKS ENGLISH! HOW WONDERFUL. THIS WILL MAKE RULING YOU FAR EASIER!
YOU WILL BE MY CHIEF SLAVE. NOW ROUND UP ALL THE LOCALS, AND THROW THEM IN A HOLE.
OH, FIRST, DIG A HOLE!
YOU DON'T UNDERSTAND - WE ALL LIVE HERE ALREADY! YOU CAN'T JUST SHOW UP AND TELL US WHAT TO DO.
THAT'S A BIT RUDE.
HMM, YOU'RE RIGHT, I'M GOING TO NEED TO USE FORCE!
FIND ME SOMETHING TO HIT YOU WITH!
OOK OOK!
ARRGH! YOU'RE NOT LISTENING TO ME AT ALL!
JAB
JAB
WHAT'S THAT? IS IT A FRUIT?
YOU! SQUIRREL! TAKE THIS ANGRY BUZZING FRUIT AND HIT YOURSELF WITH IT!
UM... OKAY.
NO, DON'T! IT'S A BEE-HIVE! THOSE ARE BEES!
BEES? WE HAVE THEM ON EARTH.
THIS IS EARTH. AND THIS IS OUR WOOD. I WON'T LET YOU TAKE IT OVER!
HA! YOU AND WHAT ARMY?
THIS ONE!
IS IT A HAT? IT'S STINGING MY HEAD!
HEE HEE HEE.
SHRIEK!
OW!
HEE HEE.
OW!
HA HA HA! MONKEY-TOPIA IS GOING TO BE BRILLIANT!
OW.
TEE HEE!
NEXT TIME - "KEEP IT DOWN!!"

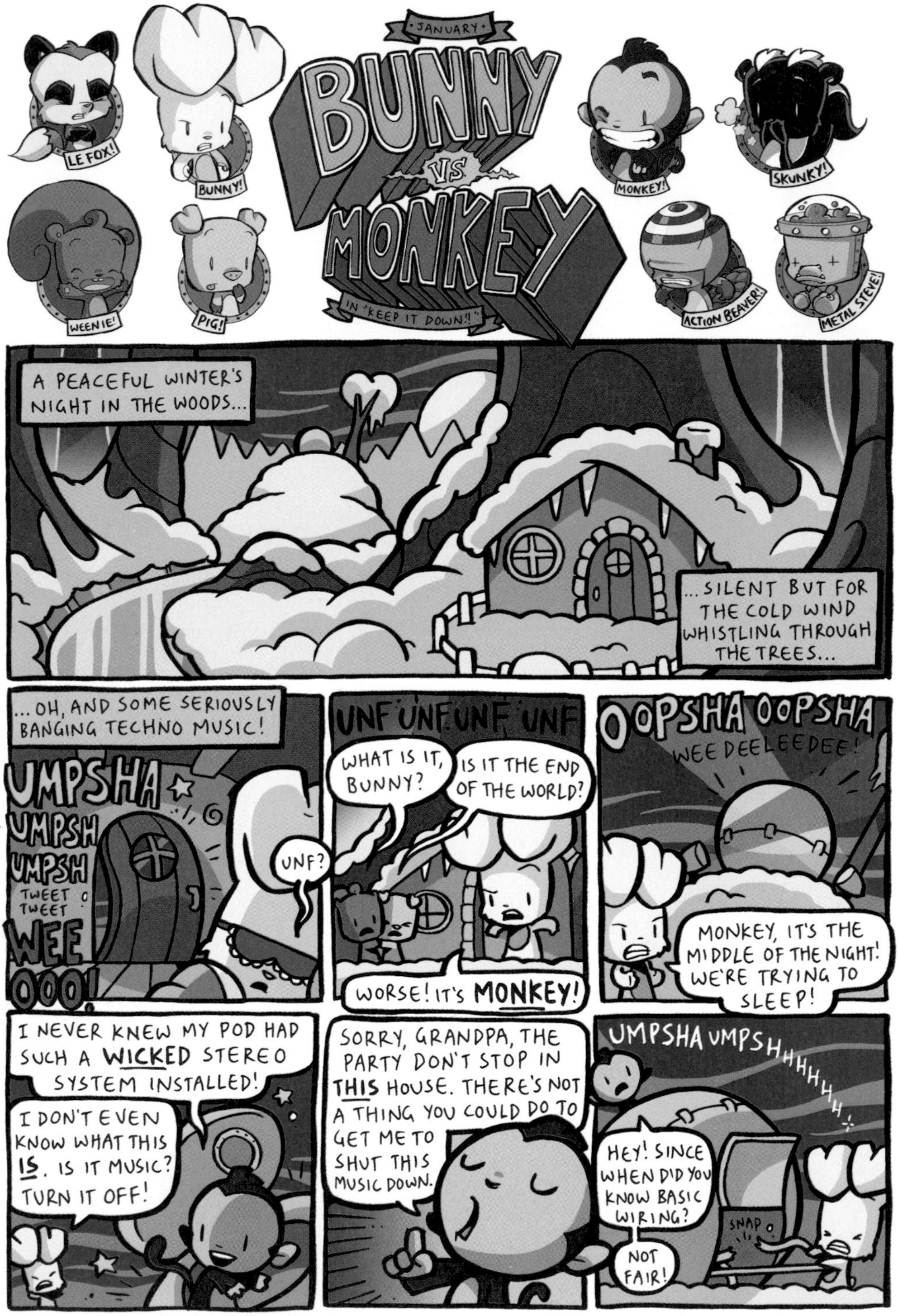

LE FOX!
BUNNY!
JANUARY
BUNNY VS MONKEY
IN "KEEP IT DOWN!"
MONKEY!
SKUNKY!
WEENIE!
PIG!
ACTION BEAVER!
METAL STEVE!
A PEACEFUL WINTER'S NIGHT IN THE WOODS...
...SILENT BUT FOR THE COLD WIND WHISTLING THROUGH THE TREES...
...OH, AND SOME SERIOUSLY BANGING TECHNO MUSIC!
UMPSHA UMPSH UMPSH TWEET TWEET WEE OOO!
UNF?
UNF UNF UNF UNF
WHAT IS IT, BUNNY?
IS IT THE END OF THE WORLD?
WORSE! IT'S MONKEY!
OOPSHA OOPSHA WEE DEELEEDEE!
MONKEY, IT'S THE MIDDLE OF THE NIGHT! WE'RE TRYING TO SLEEP!
I NEVER KNEW MY POD HAD SUCH A WICKED STEREO SYSTEM INSTALLED!
I DON'T EVEN KNOW WHAT THIS IS. IS IT MUSIC? TURN IT OFF!
SORRY, GRANDPA, THE PARTY DON'T STOP IN THIS HOUSE. THERE'S NOT A THING YOU COULD DO TO GET ME TO SHUT THIS MUSIC DOWN.
UMPSHA UMPSHHHHHH
HEY! SINCE WHEN DID YOU KNOW BASIC WIRING?
SNAP
NOT FAIR!

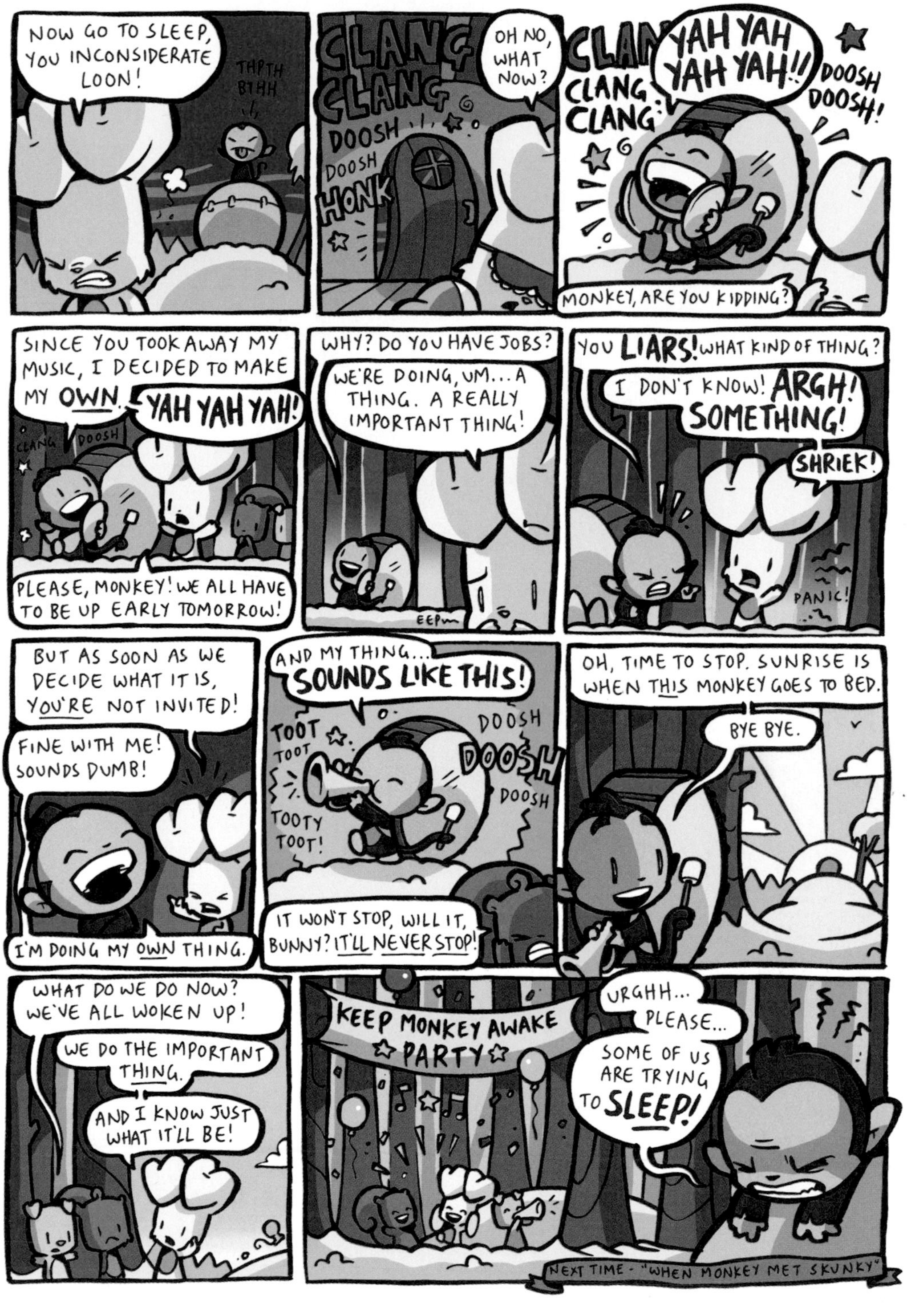

NOW GO TO SLEEP, YOU INCONSIDERATE LOON!
THPTH BTHH
CLANG CLANG
DOOSH DOOSH
HONK
OH NO, WHAT NOW?
CLANG CLANG CLANG
YAH YAH YAH YAH!!
DOOSH DOOSH!
MONKEY, ARE YOU KIDDING?
SINCE YOU TOOK AWAY MY MUSIC, I DECIDED TO MAKE MY OWN.
YAH YAH YAH!
CLANG DOOSH
PLEASE, MONKEY! WE ALL HAVE TO BE UP EARLY TOMORROW!
WHY? DO YOU HAVE JOBS?
WE'RE DOING, UM... A THING. A REALLY IMPORTANT THING!
EEP
YOU LIARS! WHAT KIND OF THING?
I DON'T KNOW! ARGH! SOMETHING!
SHRIEK!
PANIC!
BUT AS SOON AS WE DECIDE WHAT IT IS, YOU'RE NOT INVITED!
FINE WITH ME! SOUNDS DUMB!
I'M DOING MY OWN THING.
AND MY THING... SOUNDS LIKE THIS!
TOOT TOOT
TOOTY TOOT!
DOOSH DOOSH DOOSH
IT WON'T STOP, WILL IT, BUNNY? IT'LL NEVER STOP!
OH, TIME TO STOP. SUNRISE IS WHEN THIS MONKEY GOES TO BED.
BYE BYE.
WHAT DO WE DO NOW? WE'VE ALL WOKEN UP!
WE DO THE IMPORTANT THING.
AND I KNOW JUST WHAT IT'LL BE!
KEEP MONKEY AWAKE PARTY
URGHH... PLEASE...
SOME OF US ARE TRYING TO SLEEP!
NEXT TIME - "WHEN MONKEY MET SKUNKY"

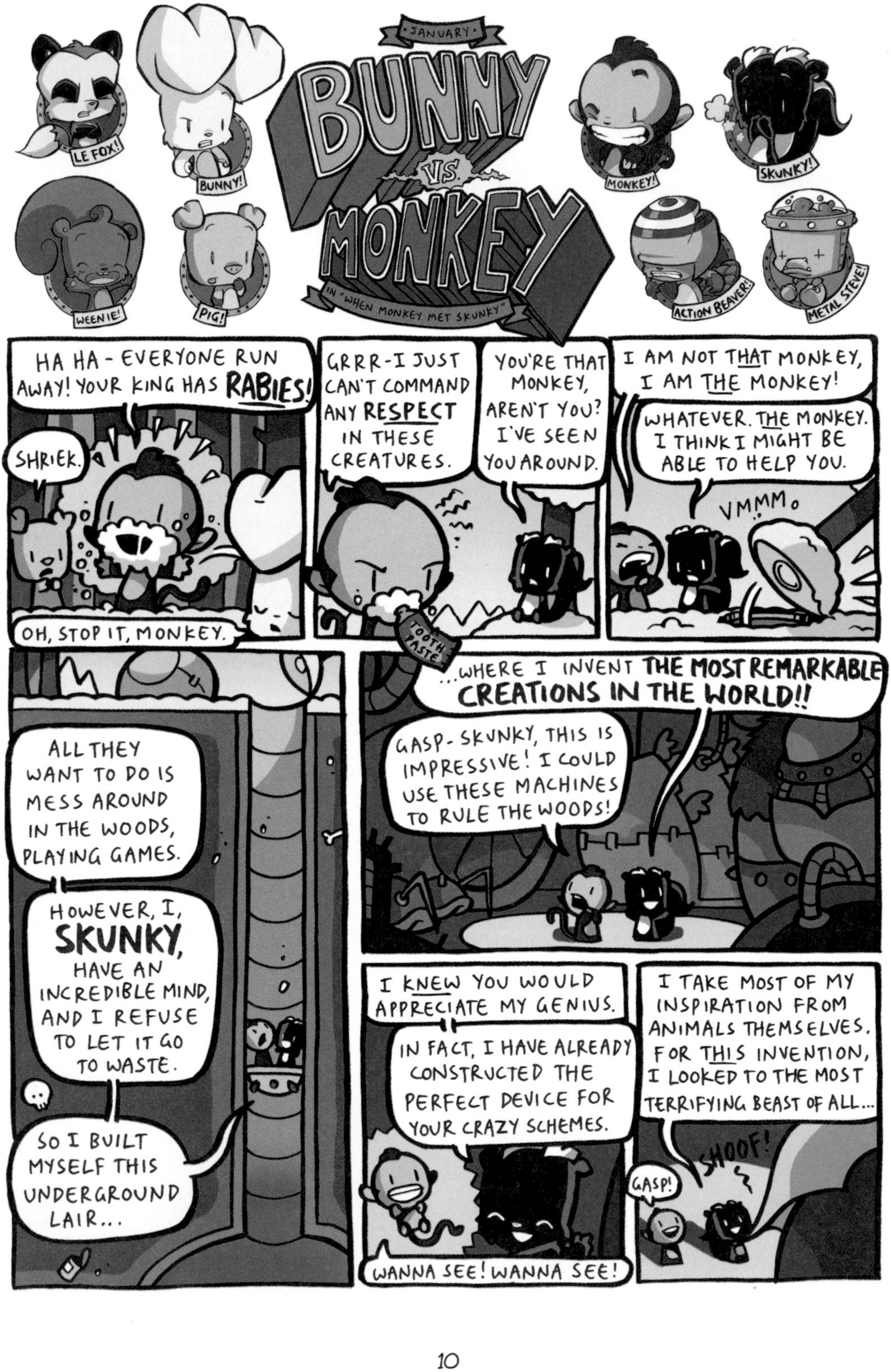
JANUARY
BUNNY VS. MONKEY
IN "WHEN MONKEY MET SKUNKY"
LE FOX!
BUNNY!
WEENIE!
PIG!
MONKEY!
SKUNKY!
ACTION BEAVER!
METAL STEVE!
HA HA - EVERYONE RUN AWAY! YOUR KING HAS RABIES!
SHRIEK.
OH, STOP IT, MONKEY.
GRRR - I JUST CAN'T COMMAND ANY RESPECT IN THESE CREATURES.
TOOTH PASTE
YOU'RE THAT MONKEY, AREN'T YOU? I'VE SEEN YOU AROUND.
I AM NOT THAT MONKEY, I AM THE MONKEY!
WHATEVER. THE MONKEY. I THINK I MIGHT BE ABLE TO HELP YOU.
VMMM
ALL THEY WANT TO DO IS MESS AROUND IN THE WOODS, PLAYING GAMES.
HOWEVER, I, SKUNKY, HAVE AN INCREDIBLE MIND, AND I REFUSE TO LET IT GO TO WASTE.
SO I BUILT MYSELF THIS UNDERGROUND LAIR...
...WHERE I INVENT THE MOST REMARKABLE CREATIONS IN THE WORLD!!
GASP - SKUNKY, THIS IS IMPRESSIVE! I COULD USE THESE MACHINES TO RULE THE WOODS!
I KNEW YOU WOULD APPRECIATE MY GENIUS.
IN FACT, I HAVE ALREADY CONSTRUCTED THE PERFECT DEVICE FOR YOUR CRAZY SCHEMES.
WANNA SEE! WANNA SEE!
I TAKE MOST OF MY INSPIRATION FROM ANIMALS THEMSELVES. FOR THIS INVENTION, I LOOKED TO THE MOST TERRIFYING BEAST OF ALL...
GASP!
SHOOF!

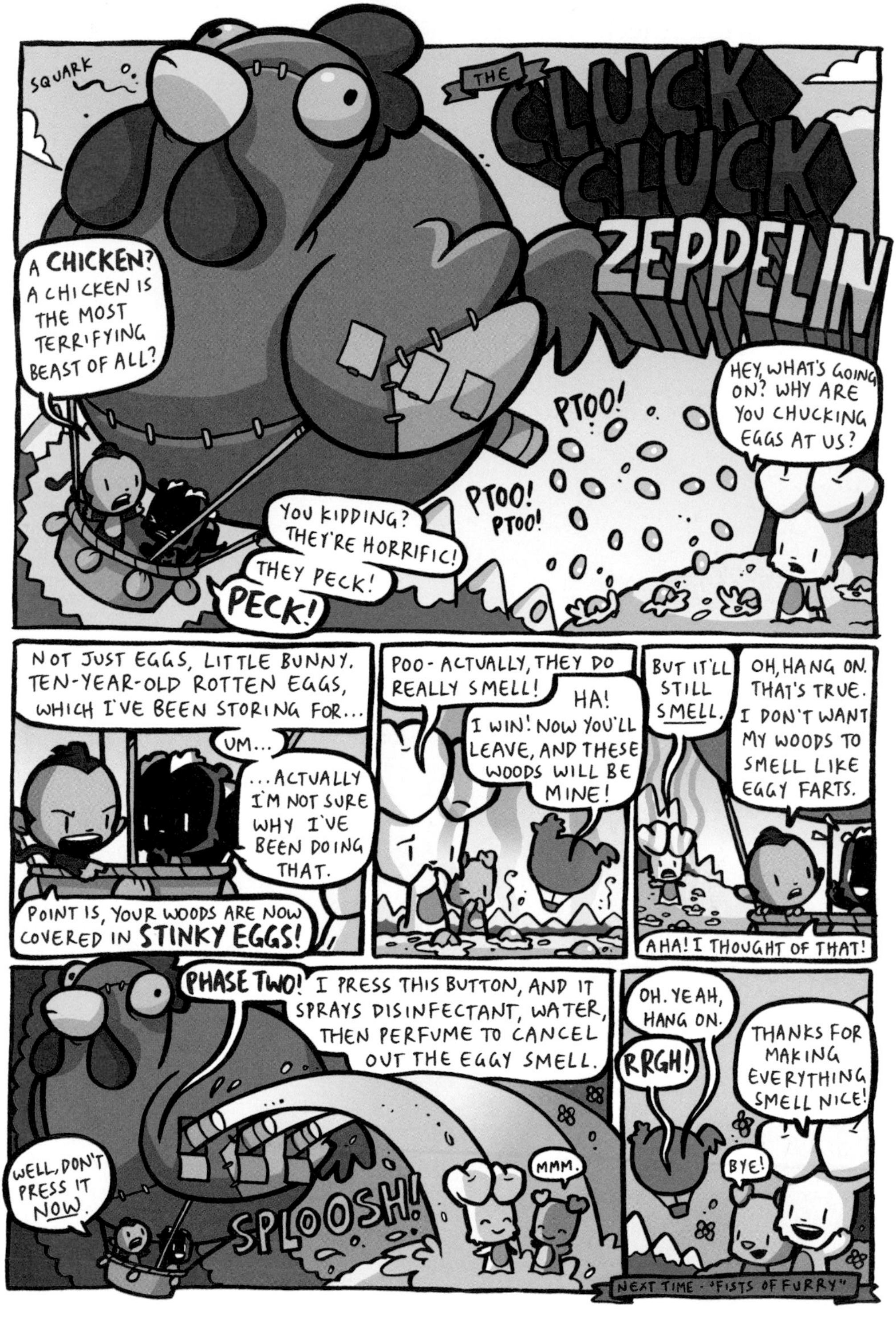
SQUARK
THE CLUCK CLUCK ZEPPELIN
A CHICKEN? A CHICKEN IS THE MOST TERRIFYING BEAST OF ALL?
YOU KIDDING? THEY'RE HORRIFIC!
THEY PECK!
PECK!
PTOO!
PTOO! PTOO!
HEY, WHAT'S GOING ON? WHY ARE YOU CHUCKING EGGS AT US?
NOT JUST EGGS, LITTLE BUNNY. TEN-YEAR-OLD ROTTEN EGGS, WHICH I'VE BEEN STORING FOR...
UM...
...ACTUALLY I'M NOT SURE WHY I'VE BEEN DOING THAT.
POINT IS, YOUR WOODS ARE NOW COVERED IN STINKY EGGS!
POO- ACTUALLY, THEY DO REALLY SMELL!
HA! I WIN! NOW YOU'LL LEAVE, AND THESE WOODS WILL BE MINE!
BUT IT'LL STILL SMELL.
OH, HANG ON. THAT'S TRUE. I DON'T WANT MY WOODS TO SMELL LIKE EGGY FARTS.
AHA! I THOUGHT OF THAT!
PHASE TWO! I PRESS THIS BUTTON, AND IT SPRAYS DISINFECTANT, WATER, THEN PERFUME TO CANCEL OUT THE EGGY SMELL.
WELL, DON'T PRESS IT NOW.
SPLOOSH!
MMM.
OH. YEAH, HANG ON.
RRGH!
THANKS FOR MAKING EVERYTHING SMELL NICE!
BYE!
NEXT TIME - "FISTS OF FURRY"

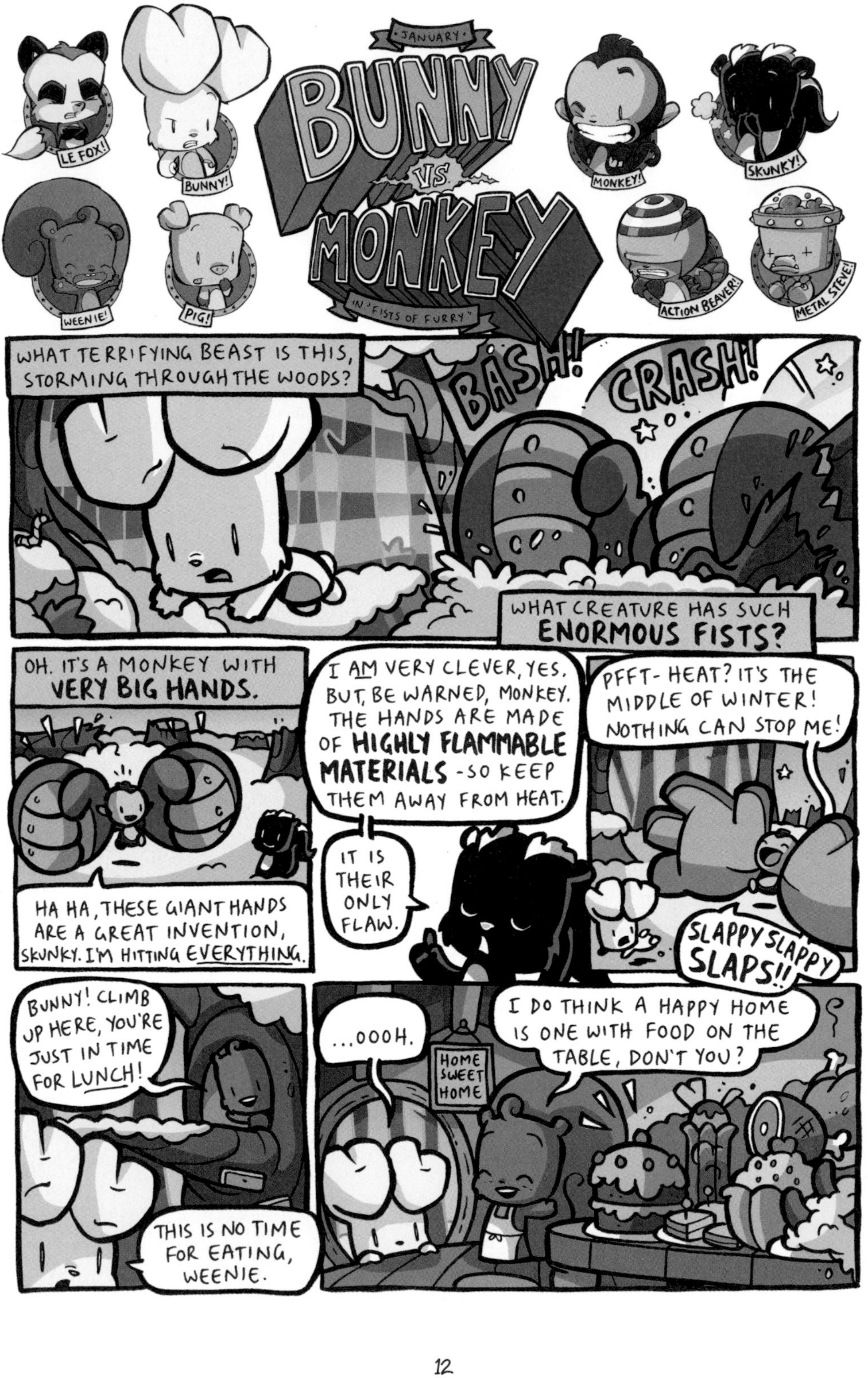
JANUARY
BUNNY VS MONKEY
IN "FISTS OF FURRY"
LE FOX!
BUNNY!
WEENIE!
PIG!
MONKEY!
SKUNKY!
ACTION BEAVER!
METAL STEVE!
WHAT TERRIFYING BEAST IS THIS, STORMING THROUGH THE WOODS?
BASH!
CRASH!
WHAT CREATURE HAS SUCH ENORMOUS FISTS?
OH. IT'S A MONKEY WITH VERY BIG HANDS.
HA HA, THESE GIANT HANDS ARE A GREAT INVENTION, SKUNKY. I'M HITTING EVERYTHING.
I AM VERY CLEVER, YES. BUT, BE WARNED, MONKEY. THE HANDS ARE MADE OF HIGHLY FLAMMABLE MATERIALS - SO KEEP THEM AWAY FROM HEAT.
IT IS THEIR ONLY FLAW.
PFFT- HEAT? IT'S THE MIDDLE OF WINTER! NOTHING CAN STOP ME!
SLAPPY SLAPPY SLAPS!!
BUNNY! CLIMB UP HERE, YOU'RE JUST IN TIME FOR LUNCH!
THIS IS NO TIME FOR EATING, WEENIE.
...OOOH.
HOME SWEET HOME
I DO THINK A HAPPY HOME IS ONE WITH FOOD ON THE TABLE, DON'T YOU?

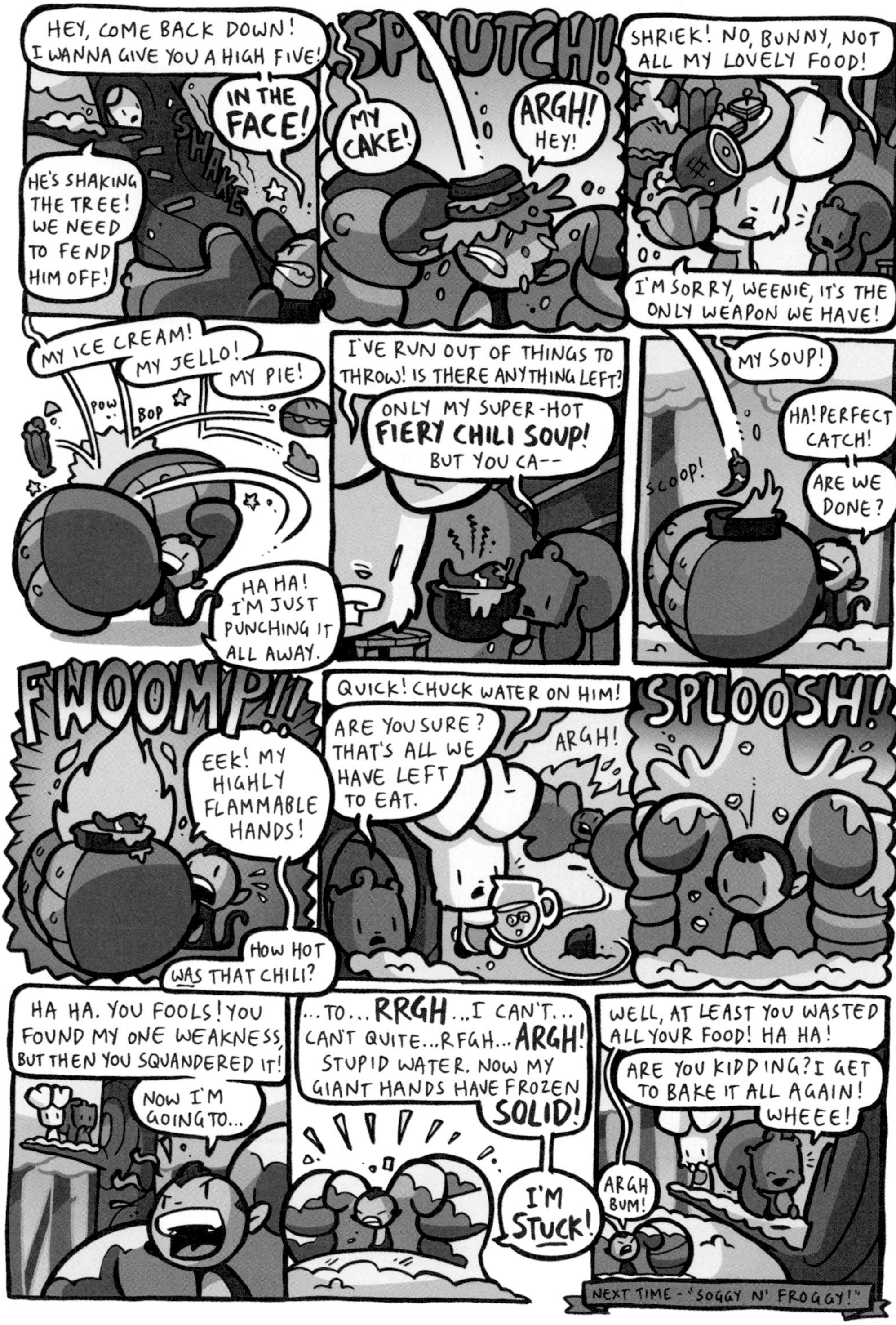
HEY, COME BACK DOWN! I WANNA GIVE YOU A HIGH FIVE!
IN THE FACE!
SHAKE
HE'S SHAKING THE TREE! WE NEED TO FEND HIM OFF!
SPLUTCH!
MY CAKE!
ARGH! HEY!
SHRIEK! NO, BUNNY, NOT ALL MY LOVELY FOOD!
I'M SORRY, WEENIE, IT'S THE ONLY WEAPON WE HAVE!
MY ICE CREAM!
MY JELLO!
MY PIE!
POW
BOP
HA HA! I'M JUST PUNCHING IT ALL AWAY.
I'VE RUN OUT OF THINGS TO THROW! IS THERE ANYTHING LEFT?
ONLY MY SUPER-HOT FIERY CHILI SOUP! BUT YOU CA--
MY SOUP!
SCOOP!
HA! PERFECT CATCH!
ARE WE DONE?
FWOOMP!!
EEK! MY HIGHLY FLAMMABLE HANDS!
HOW HOT WAS THAT CHILI?
QUICK! CHUCK WATER ON HIM!
ARE YOU SURE? THAT'S ALL WE HAVE LEFT TO EAT.
ARGH!
SPLOOSH!
HA HA. YOU FOOLS! YOU FOUND MY ONE WEAKNESS, BUT THEN YOU SQUANDERED IT!
NOW I'M GOING TO...
...TO... RRGH ...I CAN'T... CAN'T QUITE...RFGH... ARGH!
STUPID WATER. NOW MY GIANT HANDS HAVE FROZEN SOLID!
I'M STUCK!
WELL, AT LEAST YOU WASTED ALL YOUR FOOD! HA HA!
ARE YOU KIDDING? I GET TO BAKE IT ALL AGAIN! WHEEE!
ARGH BUM!
NEXT TIME - "SOGGY N' FROGGY!"

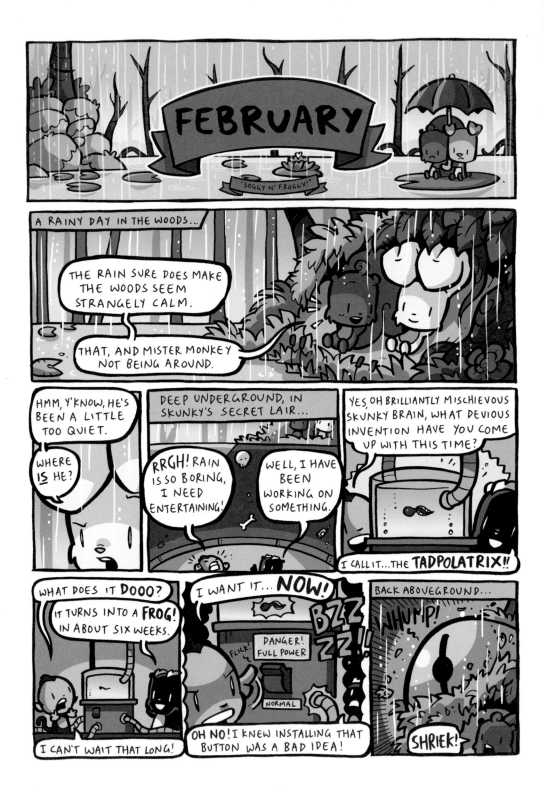

FEBRUARY

"SOGGY N' FROGGY!"

A RAINY DAY IN THE WOODS...

THE RAIN SURE DOES MAKE THE WOODS SEEM STRANGELY CALM.

THAT, AND MISTER MONKEY NOT BEING AROUND.

HMM, Y'KNOW, HE'S BEEN A LITTLE TOO QUIET.

WHERE IS HE?

DEEP UNDERGROUND, IN SKUNKY'S SECRET LAIR...

RRGH! RAIN IS SO BORING, I NEED ENTERTAINING!

WELL, I HAVE BEEN WORKING ON SOMETHING.

YES, OH BRILLIANTLY MISCHIEVOUS SKUNKY BRAIN, WHAT DEVIOUS INVENTION HAVE YOU COME UP WITH THIS TIME?

I CALL IT...THE TADPOLATRIX!!

WHAT DOES IT DOOO? IT TURNS INTO A FROG! IN ABOUT SIX WEEKS.

I CAN'T WAIT THAT LONG!

I WANT IT... NOW!

DANGER! FULL POWER

FLICK!

NORMAL

BZZZZ!!

OH NO! I KNEW INSTALLING THAT BUTTON WAS A BAD IDEA!

BACK ABOVEGROUND...

WHUMP!

SHRIEK!

14

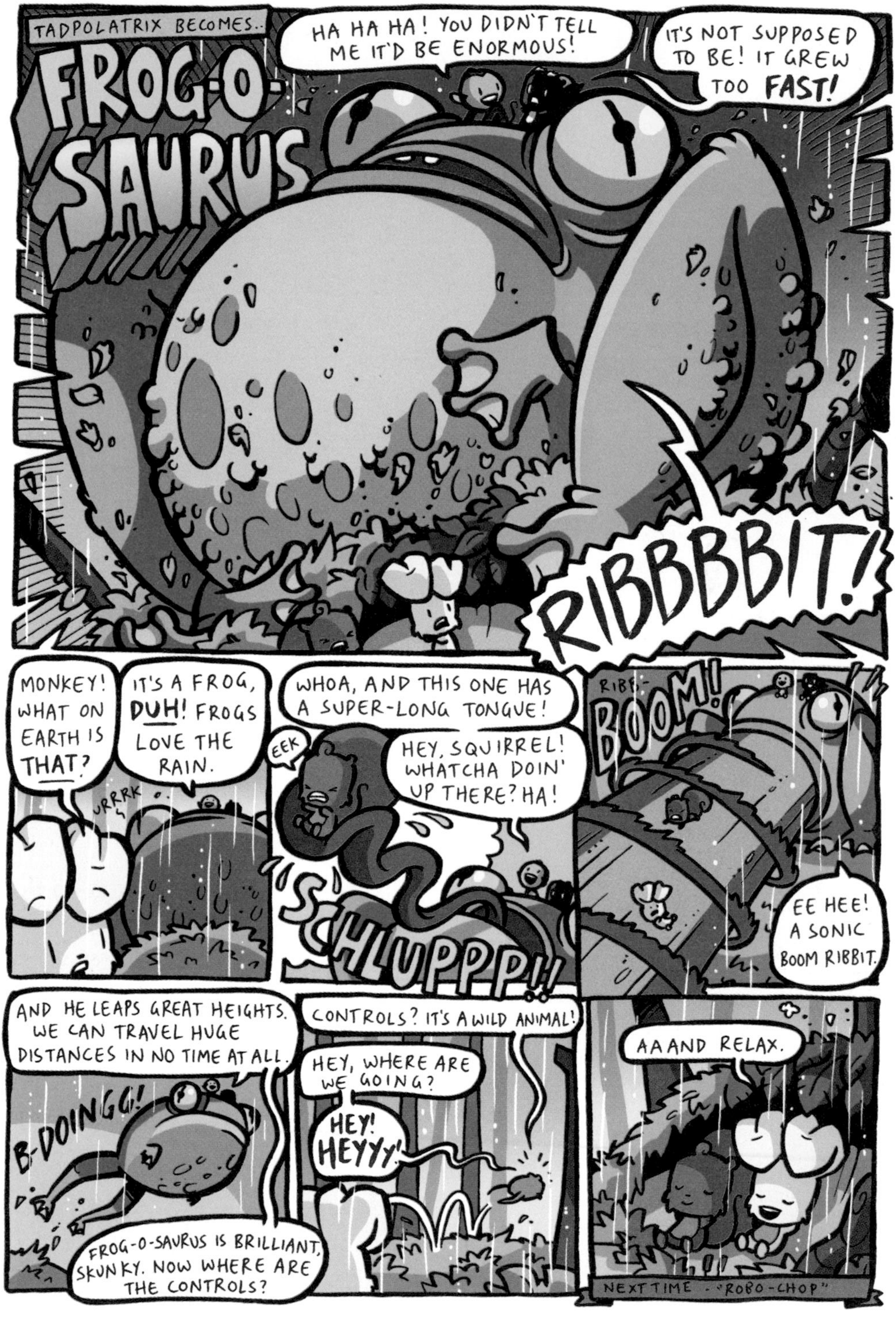

TADPOLATRIX BECOMES...
FROG-O-SAURUS
HA HA HA! YOU DIDN'T TELL ME IT'D BE ENORMOUS!
IT'S NOT SUPPOSED TO BE! IT GREW TOO FAST!
RIBBBBIT!
MONKEY! WHAT ON EARTH IS THAT?
IT'S A FROG, DUH! FROGS LOVE THE RAIN.
URRRK
WHOA, AND THIS ONE HAS A SUPER-LONG TONGUE!
EEK
HEY, SQUIRREL! WHATCHA DOIN' UP THERE? HA!
SCHLUPPPP!!
RIBB-
BOOM!
EE HEE! A SONIC BOOM RIBBIT.
AND HE LEAPS GREAT HEIGHTS. WE CAN TRAVEL HUGE DISTANCES IN NO TIME AT ALL.
B-DOINGG!
FROG-O-SAURUS IS BRILLIANT, SKUNKY. NOW WHERE ARE THE CONTROLS?
CONTROLS? IT'S A WILD ANIMAL!
HEY, WHERE ARE WE GOING?
HEY! HEYYY!
AAAND RELAX.
NEXT TIME - "ROBO-CHOP"

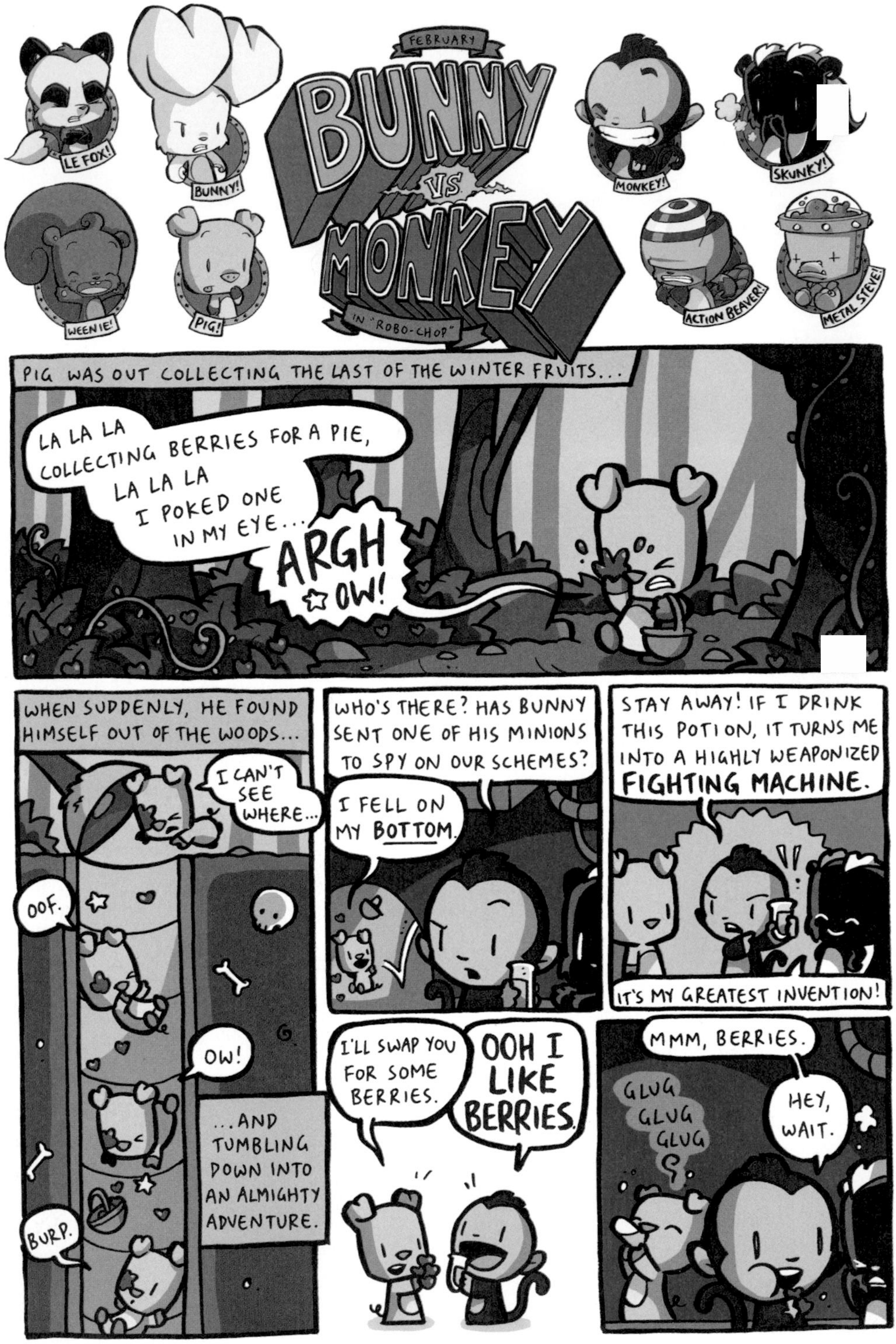

LE FOX!
BUNNY!
FEBRUARY
BUNNY VS MONKEY
IN "ROBO-CHOP"
MONKEY!
SKUNKY!
WEENIE!
PIG!
ACTION BEAVER!
METAL STEVE!
PIG WAS OUT COLLECTING THE LAST OF THE WINTER FRUITS...
LA LA LA COLLECTING BERRIES FOR A PIE, LA LA LA I POKED ONE IN MY EYE...
ARGH OW!
WHEN SUDDENLY, HE FOUND HIMSELF OUT OF THE WOODS...
I CAN'T SEE WHERE...
OOF.
OW!
BURP.
...AND TUMBLING DOWN INTO AN ALMIGHTY ADVENTURE.
WHO'S THERE? HAS BUNNY SENT ONE OF HIS MINIONS TO SPY ON OUR SCHEMES?
I FELL ON MY BOTTOM.
STAY AWAY! IF I DRINK THIS POTION, IT TURNS ME INTO A HIGHLY WEAPONIZED FIGHTING MACHINE.
IT'S MY GREATEST INVENTION!
I'LL SWAP YOU FOR SOME BERRIES.
OOH I LIKE BERRIES.
MMM, BERRIES.
GLUG GLUG GLUG
HEY, WAIT.

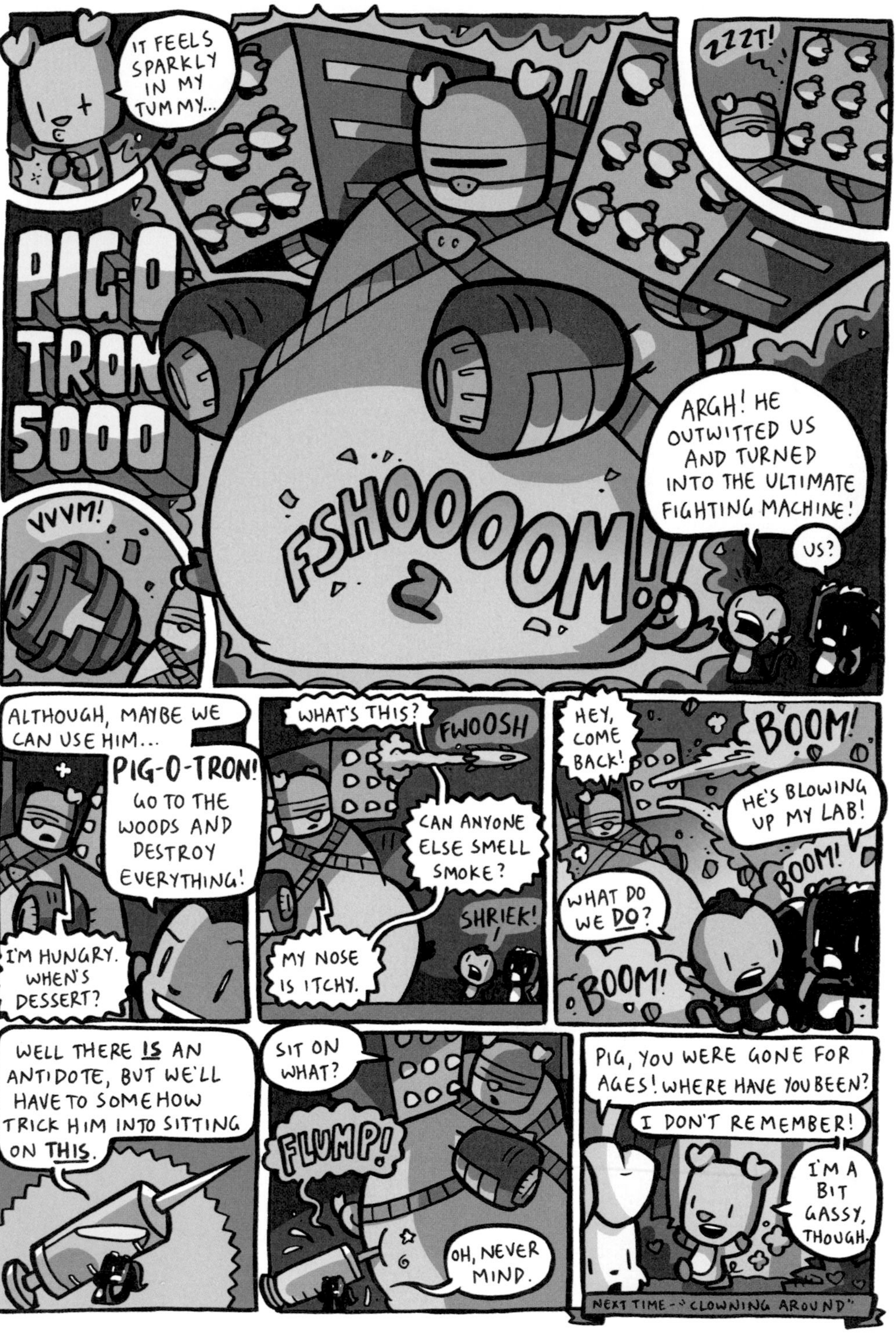
IT FEELS SPARKLY IN MY TUMMY...
ZZZT!
PIG-O-TRON 5000
VVVM!
FSHOOOOOM!!!
ARGH! HE OUTWITTED US AND TURNED INTO THE ULTIMATE FIGHTING MACHINE!
US?
ALTHOUGH, MAYBE WE CAN USE HIM...
PIG-O-TRON! GO TO THE WOODS AND DESTROY EVERYTHING!
I'M HUNGRY. WHEN'S DESSERT?
WHAT'S THIS?
FWOOSH
CAN ANYONE ELSE SMELL SMOKE?
SHRIEK!
MY NOSE IS ITCHY.
HEY, COME BACK!
BOOM!
HE'S BLOWING UP MY LAB!
BOOM!
WHAT DO WE DO?
BOOM!
WELL THERE IS AN ANTIDOTE, BUT WE'LL HAVE TO SOMEHOW TRICK HIM INTO SITTING ON THIS.
SIT ON WHAT?
FLUMP!
OH, NEVER MIND.
PIG, YOU WERE GONE FOR AGES! WHERE HAVE YOU BEEN?
I DON'T REMEMBER!
I'M A BIT GASSY, THOUGH.
NEXT TIME - "CLOWNING AROUND"

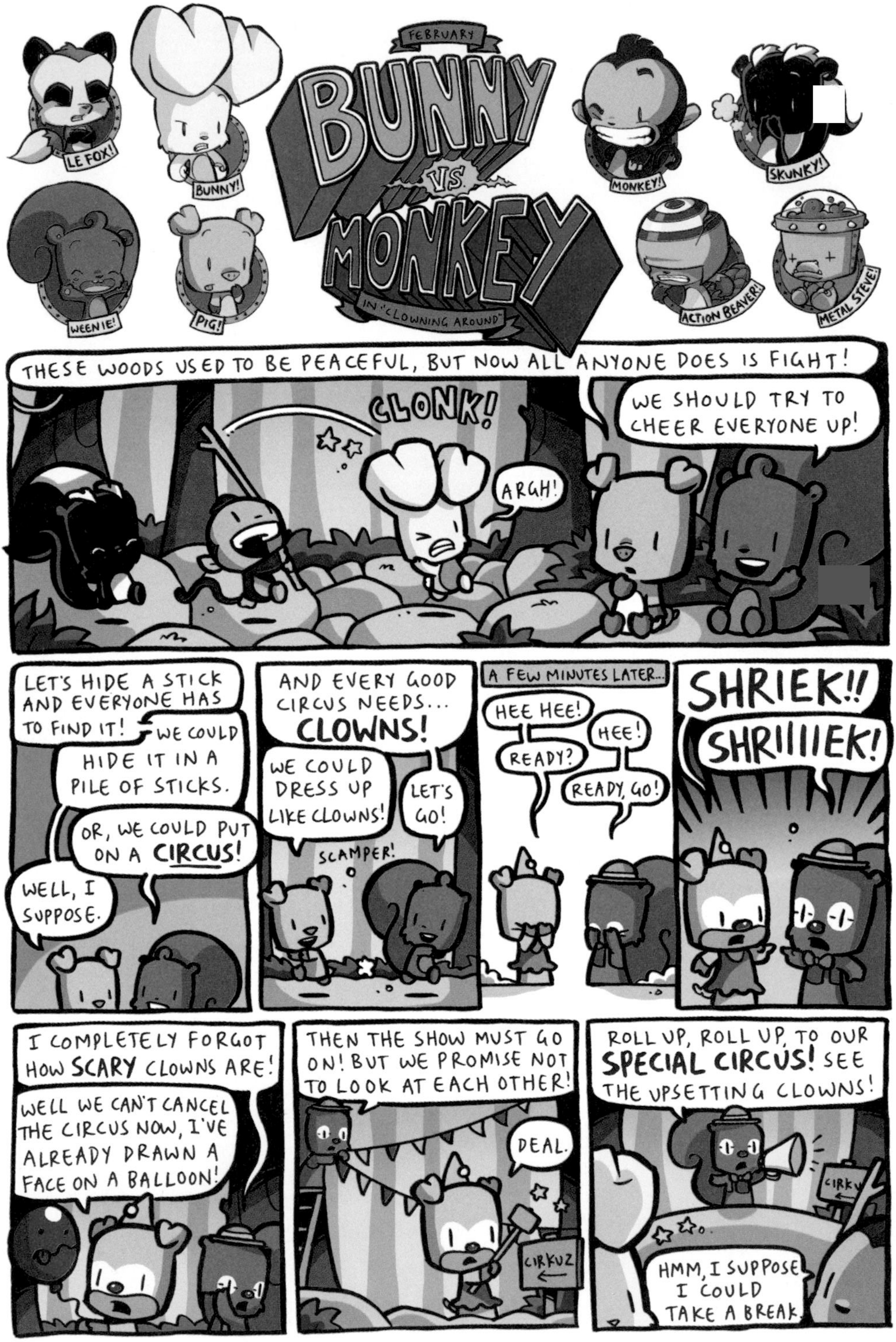
LE FOX!
BUNNY!
FEBRUARY
BUNNY VS MONKEY
IN "CLOWNING AROUND"
MONKEY!
SKUNKY!
WEENIE!
PIG!
ACTION BEAVER!
METAL STEVE!
THESE WOODS USED TO BE PEACEFUL, BUT NOW ALL ANYONE DOES IS FIGHT!
CLONK!
ARGH!
WE SHOULD TRY TO CHEER EVERYONE UP!
LET'S HIDE A STICK AND EVERYONE HAS TO FIND IT!
WE COULD HIDE IT IN A PILE OF STICKS.
OR, WE COULD PUT ON A CIRCUS!
WELL, I SUPPOSE.
AND EVERY GOOD CIRCUS NEEDS... CLOWNS!
WE COULD DRESS UP LIKE CLOWNS!
LET'S GO!
SCAMPER!
A FEW MINUTES LATER...
HEE HEE!
HEE!
READY?
READY, GO!
SHRIEK!!
SHRIIIIEK!
I COMPLETELY FORGOT HOW SCARY CLOWNS ARE!
WELL WE CAN'T CANCEL THE CIRCUS NOW, I'VE ALREADY DRAWN A FACE ON A BALLOON!
THEN THE SHOW MUST GO ON! BUT WE PROMISE NOT TO LOOK AT EACH OTHER!
DEAL.
CIRKUZ
ROLL UP, ROLL UP, TO OUR SPECIAL CIRCUS! SEE THE UPSETTING CLOWNS!
CIRKY
HMM, I SUPPOSE I COULD TAKE A BREAK.

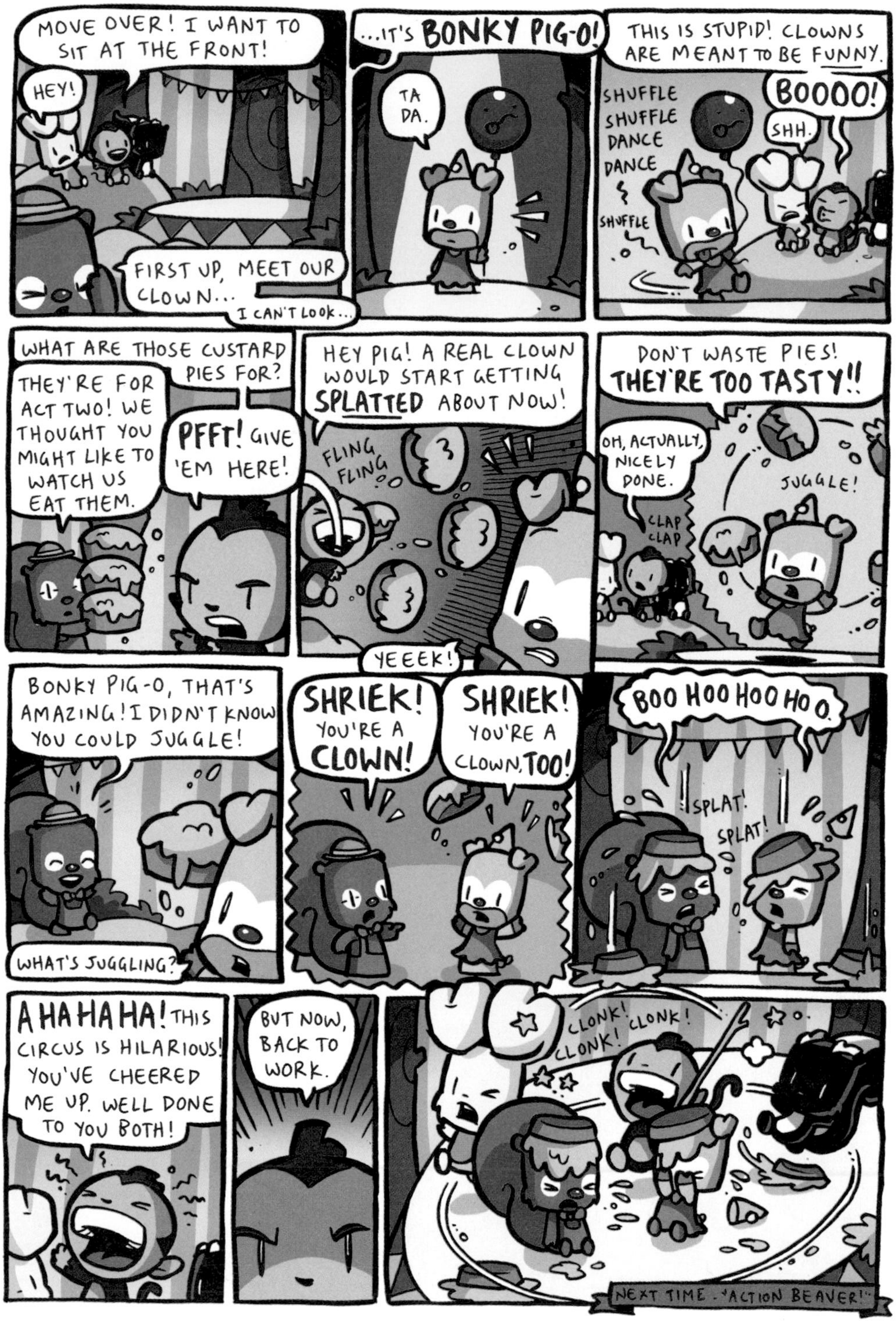
MOVE OVER! I WANT TO SIT AT THE FRONT!
HEY!
FIRST UP, MEET OUR CLOWN...
I CAN'T LOOK...
...IT'S BONKY PIG-O!
TA DA.
THIS IS STUPID! CLOWNS ARE MEANT TO BE FUNNY.
BOOOO!
SHH.
SHUFFLE SHUFFLE DANCE DANCE
SHUFFLE
WHAT ARE THOSE CUSTARD PIES FOR?
THEY'RE FOR ACT TWO! WE THOUGHT YOU MIGHT LIKE TO WATCH US EAT THEM.
PFFT! GIVE 'EM HERE!
HEY PIG! A REAL CLOWN WOULD START GETTING SPLATTED ABOUT NOW!
FLING FLING
YEEEK!
DON'T WASTE PIES! THEY'RE TOO TASTY!!
OH, ACTUALLY, NICELY DONE.
CLAP CLAP
JUGGLE!
BONKY PIG-O, THAT'S AMAZING! I DIDN'T KNOW YOU COULD JUGGLE!
WHAT'S JUGGLING?
SHRIEK! YOU'RE A CLOWN!
SHRIEK! YOU'RE A CLOWN, TOO!
BOO HOO HOO HO O.
SPLAT!
SPLAT!
AHAHAHA! THIS CIRCUS IS HILARIOUS! YOU'VE CHEERED ME UP. WELL DONE TO YOU BOTH!
BUT NOW, BACK TO WORK.
CLONK! CLONK! CLONK!
NEXT TIME - "ACTION BEAVER!"

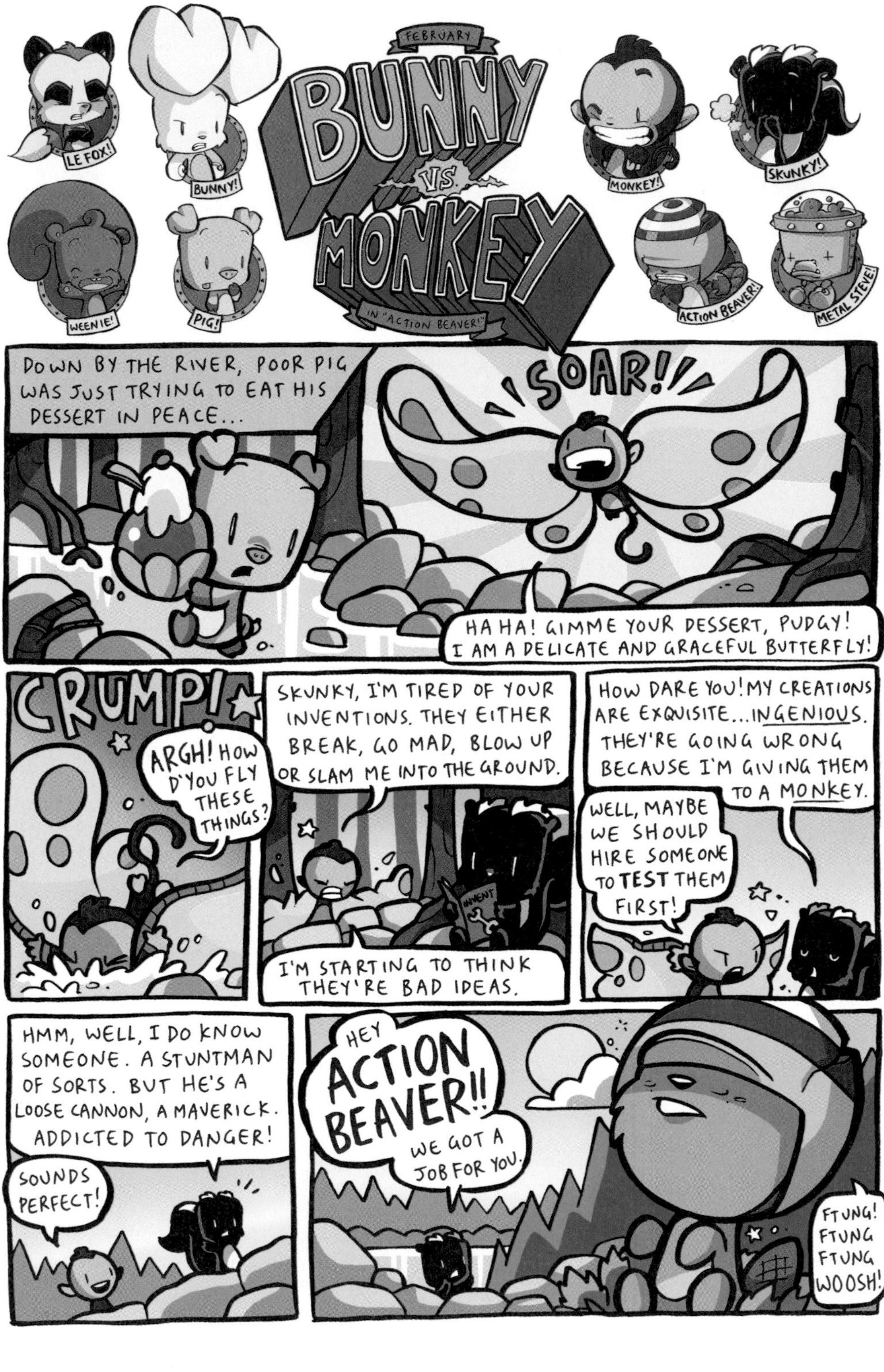
LE FOX!
BUNNY!
WEENIE!
PIG!
FEBRUARY
BUNNY VS MONKEY
IN "ACTION BEAVER!"
MONKEY!
SKUNKY!
ACTION BEAVER!
METAL STEVE!
DOWN BY THE RIVER, POOR PIG WAS JUST TRYING TO EAT HIS DESSERT IN PEACE...
SOAR!!
HA HA! GIMME YOUR DESSERT, PUDGY! I AM A DELICATE AND GRACEFUL BUTTERFLY!
CRUMP!
ARGH! HOW D'YOU FLY THESE THINGS?
SKUNKY, I'M TIRED OF YOUR INVENTIONS. THEY EITHER BREAK, GO MAD, BLOW UP OR SLAM ME INTO THE GROUND.
I'M STARTING TO THINK THEY'RE BAD IDEAS.
HOW DARE YOU! MY CREATIONS ARE EXQUISITE... INGENIOUS. THEY'RE GOING WRONG BECAUSE I'M GIVING THEM TO A MONKEY.
WELL, MAYBE WE SHOULD HIRE SOMEONE TO TEST THEM FIRST!
HMM, WELL, I DO KNOW SOMEONE. A STUNTMAN OF SORTS. BUT HE'S A LOOSE CANNON, A MAVERICK. ADDICTED TO DANGER!
SOUNDS PERFECT!
HEY ACTION BEAVER!!
WE GOT A JOB FOR YOU.
FTUNG! FTUNG FTUNG WOOSH!

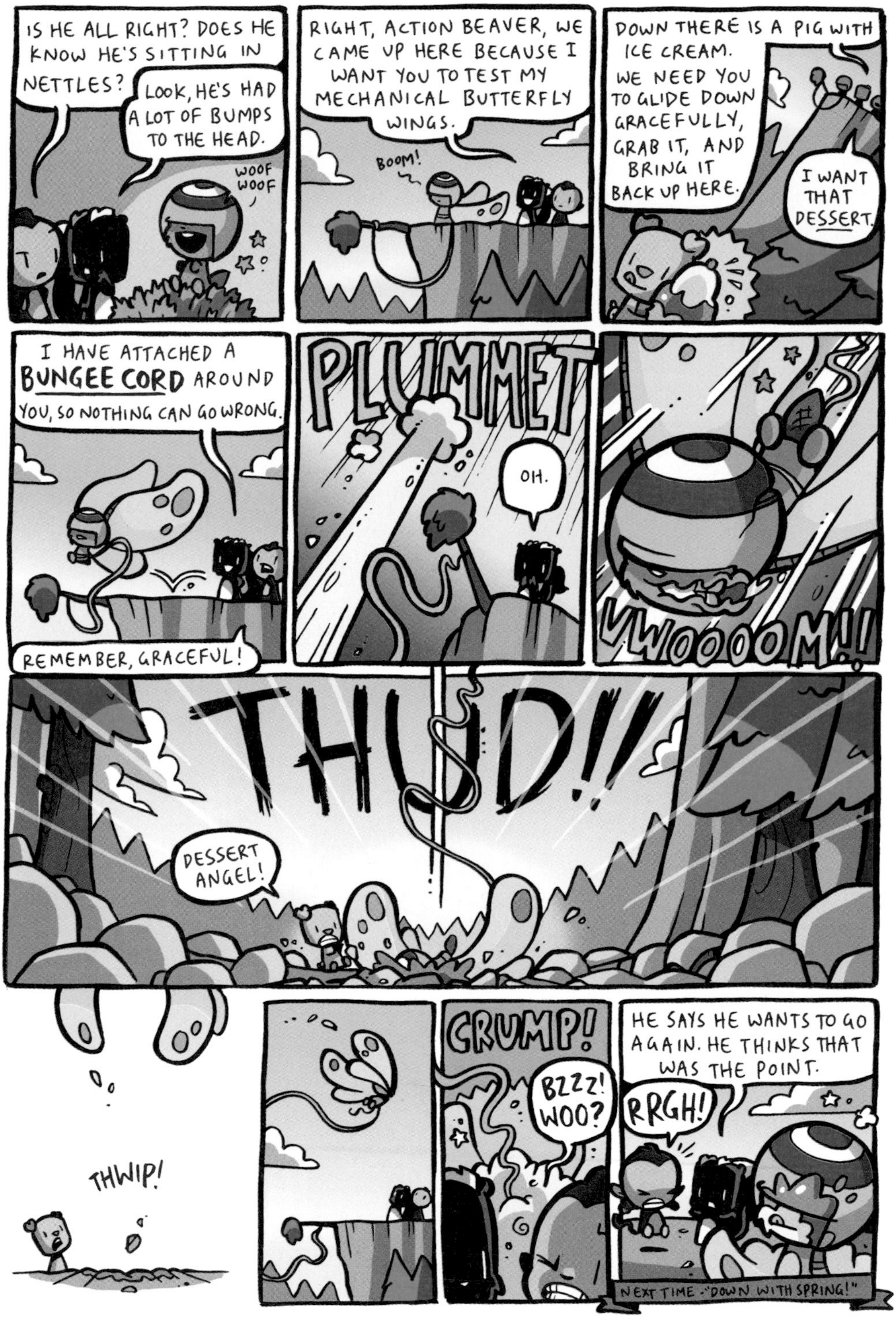
IS HE ALL RIGHT? DOES HE KNOW HE'S SITTING IN NETTLES?
LOOK, HE'S HAD A LOT OF BUMPS TO THE HEAD.
WOOF WOOF
RIGHT, ACTION BEAVER, WE CAME UP HERE BECAUSE I WANT YOU TO TEST MY MECHANICAL BUTTERFLY WINGS.
BOOM!
DOWN THERE IS A PIG WITH ICE CREAM.
WE NEED YOU TO GLIDE DOWN GRACEFULLY, GRAB IT, AND BRING IT BACK UP HERE.
I WANT THAT DESSERT.
I HAVE ATTACHED A BUNGEE CORD AROUND YOU, SO NOTHING CAN GO WRONG.
REMEMBER, GRACEFUL!
PLUMMET
OH.
VWOOOOOM!!
THUD!!
DESSERT ANGEL!
THWIP!
CRUMP!
BZZZ! WOO?
HE SAYS HE WANTS TO GO AGAIN. HE THINKS THAT WAS THE POINT.
RRGH!
NEXT TIME - "DOWN WITH SPRING!"

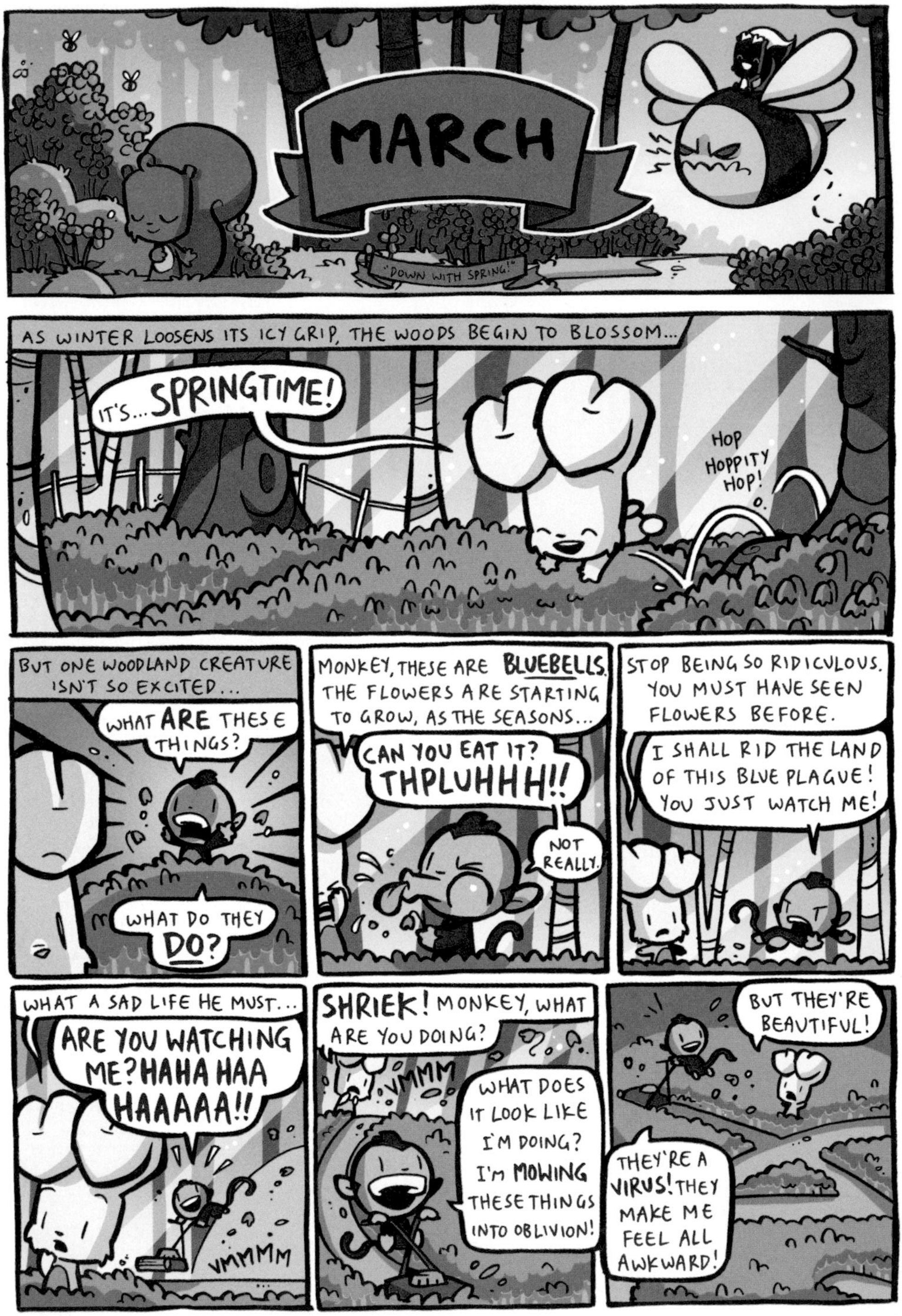
MARCH
"DOWN WITH SPRING!"
AS WINTER LOOSENS ITS ICY GRIP, THE WOODS BEGIN TO BLOSSOM...
IT'S... SPRINGTIME!
HOP HOPPITY HOP!
BUT ONE WOODLAND CREATURE ISN'T SO EXCITED...
WHAT ARE THESE THINGS?
WHAT DO THEY DO?
MONKEY, THESE ARE BLUEBELLS. THE FLOWERS ARE STARTING TO GROW, AS THE SEASONS...
CAN YOU EAT IT? THPLUHHH!!
NOT REALLY.
STOP BEING SO RIDICULOUS. YOU MUST HAVE SEEN FLOWERS BEFORE.
I SHALL RID THE LAND OF THIS BLUE PLAGUE! YOU JUST WATCH ME!
WHAT A SAD LIFE HE MUST...
ARE YOU WATCHING ME? HAHA HAA HAAAAA!!
VMMMM
SHRIEK! MONKEY, WHAT ARE YOU DOING?
VMMM
WHAT DOES IT LOOK LIKE I'M DOING? I'M MOWING THESE THINGS INTO OBLIVION!
BUT THEY'RE BEAUTIFUL!
THEY'RE A VIRUS! THEY MAKE ME FEEL ALL AWKWARD!

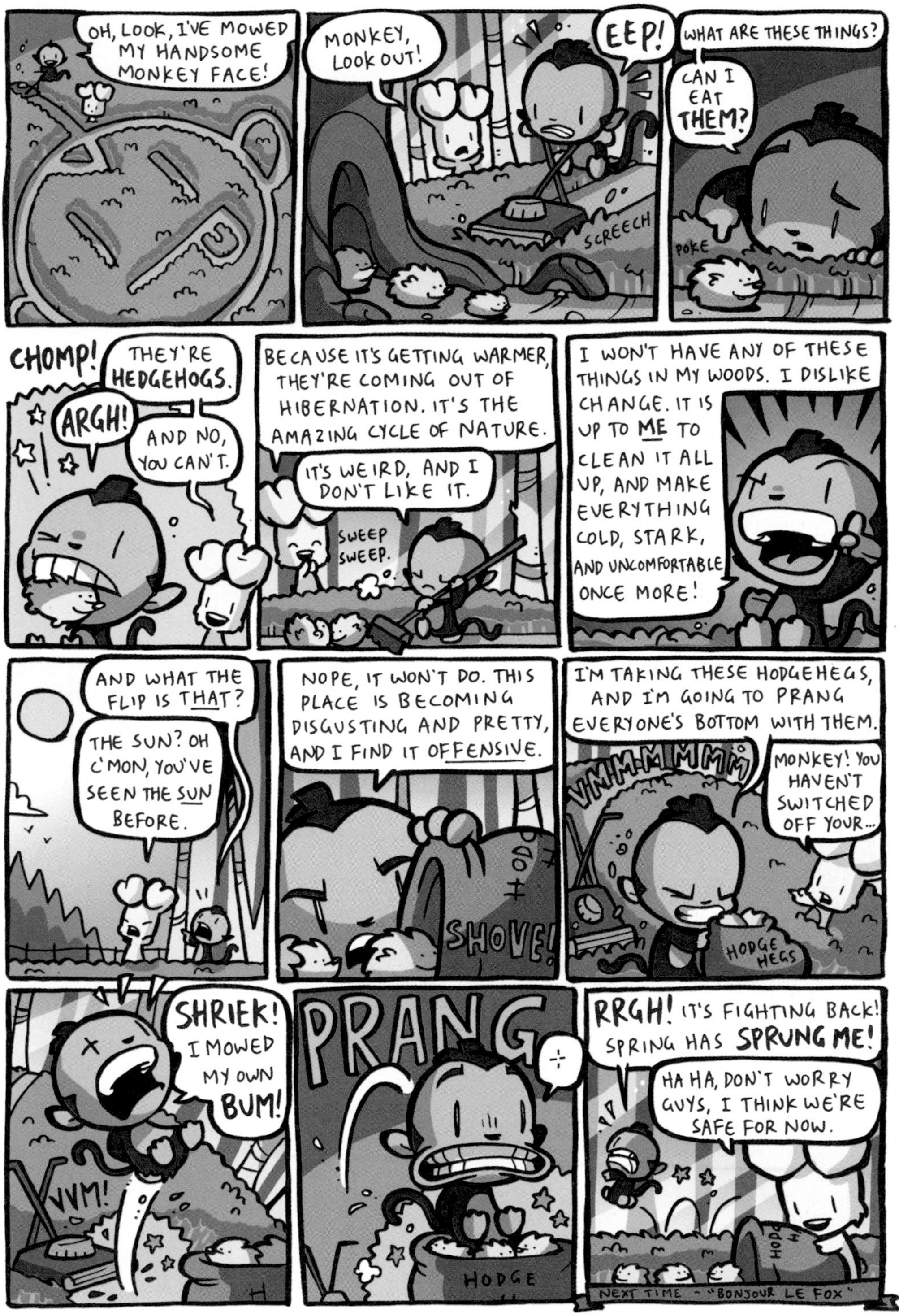
OH, LOOK, I'VE MOWED MY HANDSOME MONKEY FACE!
MONKEY, LOOK OUT!
EEP!
SCREECH
WHAT ARE THESE THINGS?
CAN I EAT THEM?
POKE
CHOMP!
THEY'RE HEDGEHOGS.
ARGH!
AND NO, YOU CAN'T.
BECAUSE IT'S GETTING WARMER, THEY'RE COMING OUT OF HIBERNATION. IT'S THE AMAZING CYCLE OF NATURE.
IT'S WEIRD, AND I DON'T LIKE IT.
SWEEP SWEEP.
I WON'T HAVE ANY OF THESE THINGS IN MY WOODS. I DISLIKE CHANGE. IT IS UP TO ME TO CLEAN IT ALL UP, AND MAKE EVERYTHING COLD, STARK, AND UNCOMFORTABLE ONCE MORE!
AND WHAT THE FLIP IS THAT?
THE SUN? OH C'MON, YOU'VE SEEN THE SUN BEFORE.
NOPE, IT WON'T DO. THIS PLACE IS BECOMING DISGUSTING AND PRETTY, AND I FIND IT OFFENSIVE.
SHOVE!
I'M TAKING THESE HODGEHEGS, AND I'M GOING TO PRANG EVERYONE'S BOTTOM WITH THEM.
VMMMMMMMM
MONKEY! YOU HAVEN'T SWITCHED OFF YOUR...
HODGE HEGS
SHRIEK! I MOWED MY OWN BUM!
VVM!
PRANG
HODGE
RRGH! IT'S FIGHTING BACK! SPRING HAS SPRUNG ME!
HA HA, DON'T WORRY GUYS, I THINK WE'RE SAFE FOR NOW.
NEXT TIME - "BONJOUR LE FOX"

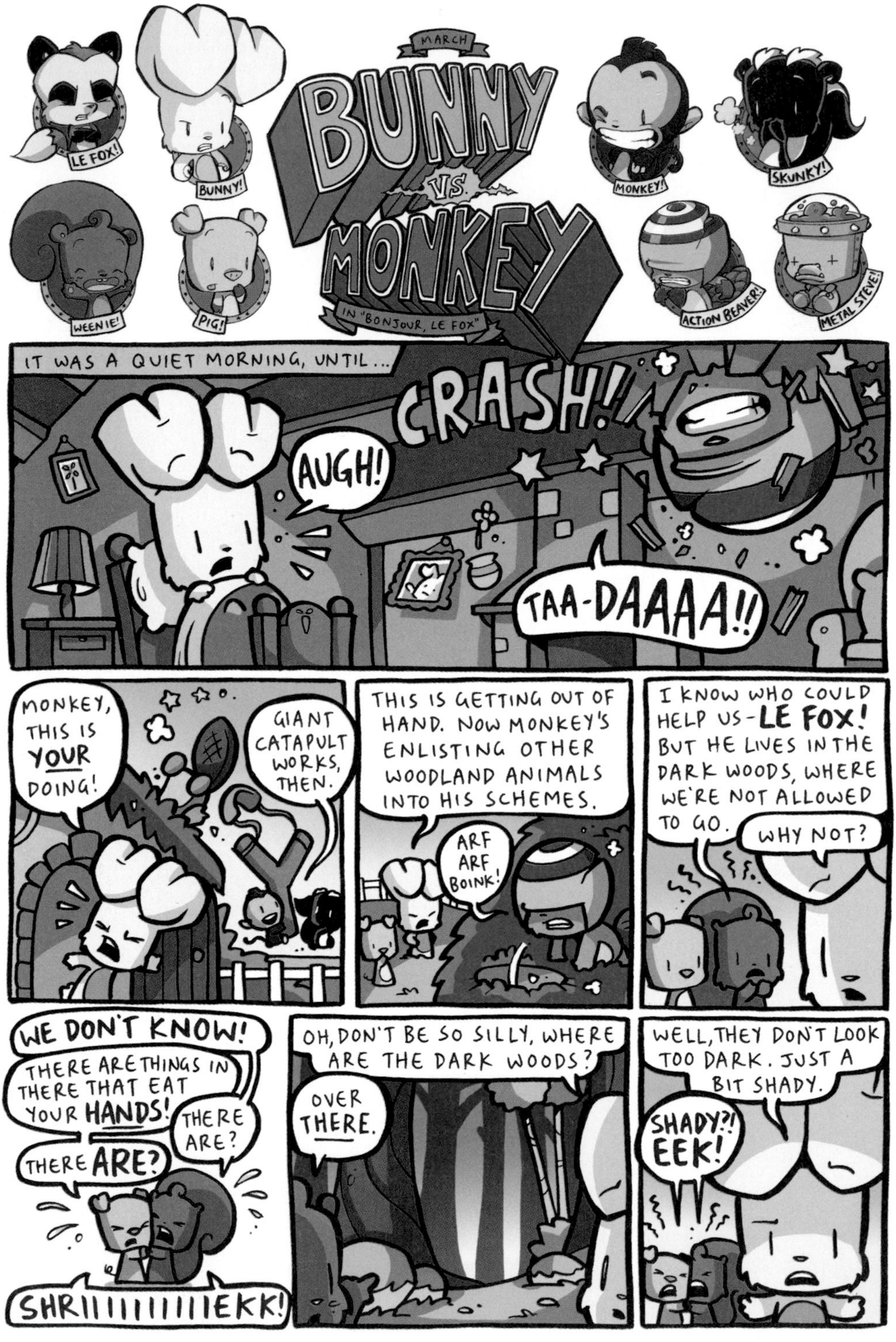
MARCH
BUNNY VS. MONKEY
IN "BONJOUR, LE FOX"
LE FOX!
BUNNY!
WEENIE!
PIG!
MONKEY!
SKUNKY!
ACTION BEAVER!
METAL STEVE!
IT WAS A QUIET MORNING, UNTIL...
CRASH!
AUGH!
TAA-DAAAA!!
MONKEY, THIS IS YOUR DOING!
GIANT CATAPULT WORKS, THEN.
THIS IS GETTING OUT OF HAND. NOW MONKEY'S ENLISTING OTHER WOODLAND ANIMALS INTO HIS SCHEMES.
ARF ARF BOINK!
I KNOW WHO COULD HELP US - LE FOX! BUT HE LIVES IN THE DARK WOODS, WHERE WE'RE NOT ALLOWED TO GO.
WHY NOT?
WE DON'T KNOW!
THERE ARE THINGS IN THERE THAT EAT YOUR HANDS!
THERE ARE?
THERE ARE?
SHRIIIIIIIIIIEKK!
OH, DON'T BE SO SILLY, WHERE ARE THE DARK WOODS?
OVER THERE.
WELL, THEY DON'T LOOK TOO DARK. JUST A BIT SHADY.
SHADY?! EEK!

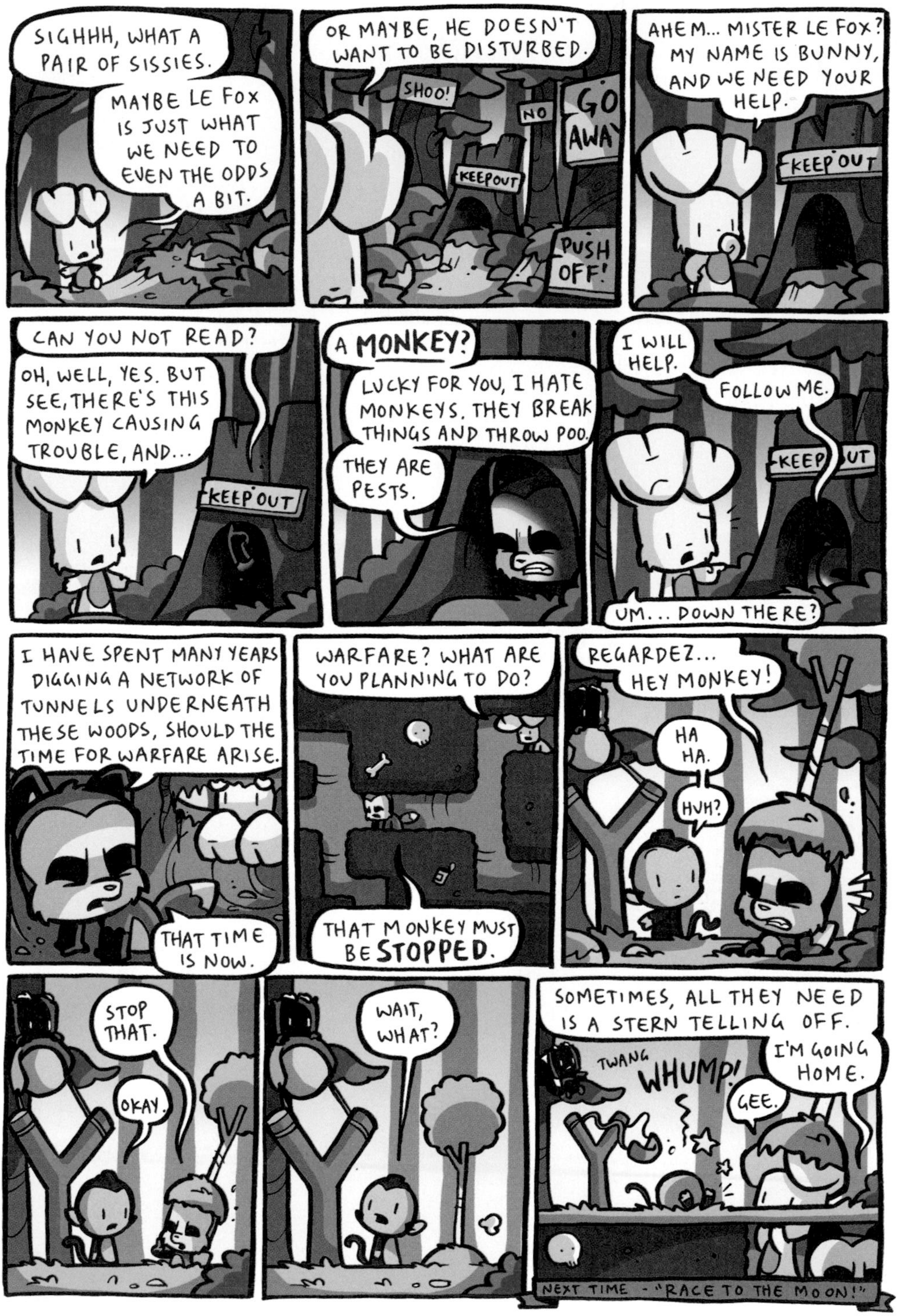
SIGHHH, WHAT A PAIR OF SISSIES.
MAYBE LE FOX IS JUST WHAT WE NEED TO EVEN THE ODDS A BIT.
OR MAYBE, HE DOESN'T WANT TO BE DISTURBED.
SHOO!
NO
GO AWAY
KEEP OUT
PUSH OFF!
AHEM... MISTER LE FOX? MY NAME IS BUNNY, AND WE NEED YOUR HELP.
KEEP OUT
CAN YOU NOT READ?
OH, WELL, YES. BUT SEE, THERE'S THIS MONKEY CAUSING TROUBLE, AND...
KEEP OUT
A **MONKEY**?
LUCKY FOR YOU, I HATE MONKEYS. THEY BREAK THINGS AND THROW POO.
THEY ARE PESTS.
I WILL HELP.
FOLLOW ME.
UM... DOWN THERE?
I HAVE SPENT MANY YEARS DIGGING A NETWORK OF TUNNELS UNDERNEATH THESE WOODS, SHOULD THE TIME FOR WARFARE ARISE.
THAT TIME IS NOW.
WARFARE? WHAT ARE YOU PLANNING TO DO?
THAT MONKEY MUST BE **STOPPED**.
REGARDEZ...
HEY MONKEY!
HA HA.
HUH?
STOP THAT.
OKAY.
WAIT, WHAT?
SOMETIMES, ALL THEY NEED IS A STERN TELLING OFF.
TWANG
WHUMP!
I'M GOING HOME.
GEE.
NEXT TIME - "RACE TO THE MOON!"

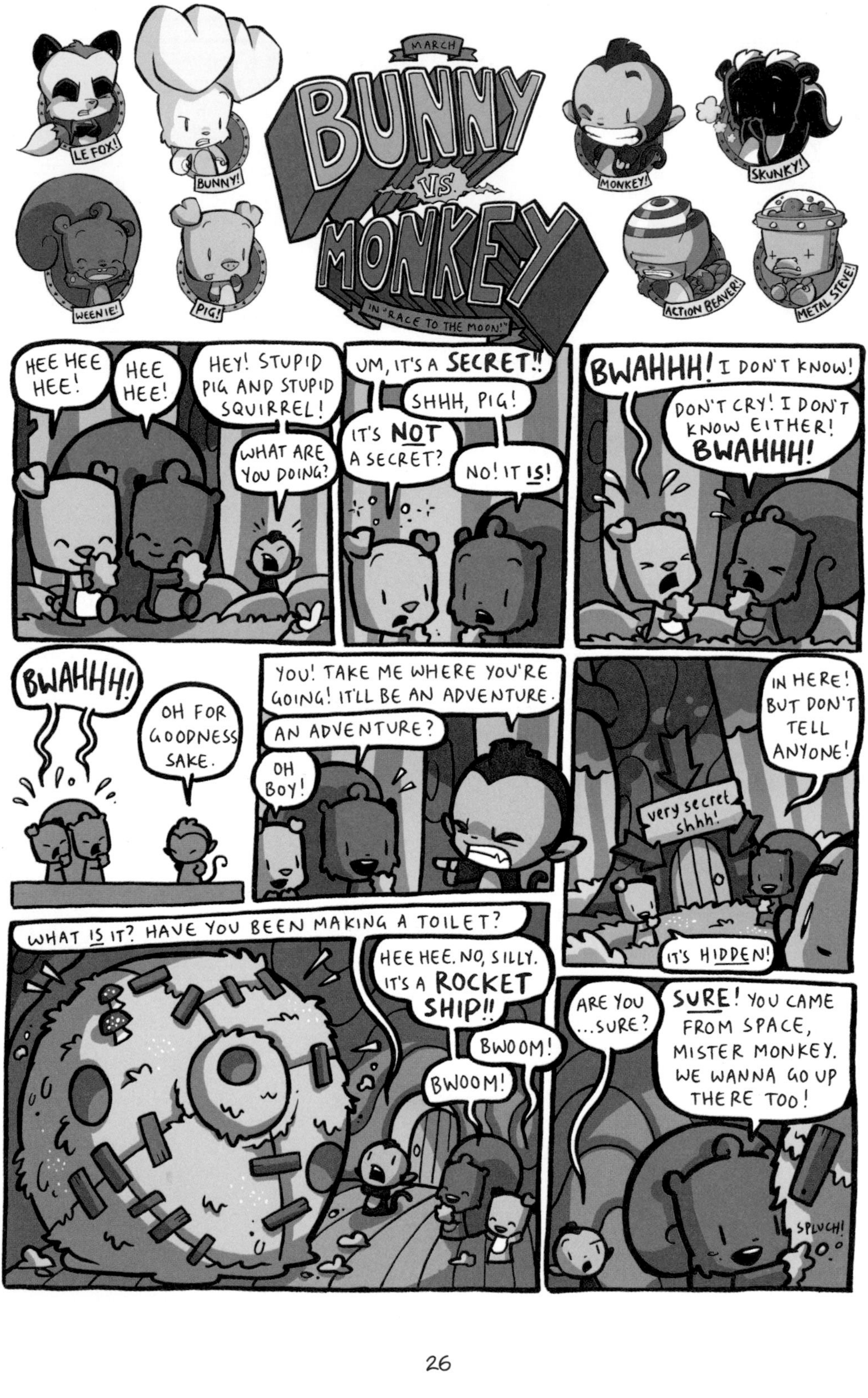

MARCH
BUNNY VS MONKEY
IN "RACE TO THE MOON!"
LE FOX!
BUNNY!
WEENIE!
PIG!
MONKEY!
SKUNKY!
ACTION BEAVER!
METAL STEVE!
HEE HEE HEE!
HEE HEE!
HEY! STUPID PIG AND STUPID SQUIRREL!
WHAT ARE YOU DOING?
UM, IT'S A SECRET!!
SHHH, PIG!
IT'S NOT A SECRET?
NO! IT IS!
BWAHHH! I DON'T KNOW!
DON'T CRY! I DON'T KNOW EITHER! BWAHHH!
BWAHHH!
OH FOR GOODNESS SAKE.
YOU! TAKE ME WHERE YOU'RE GOING! IT'LL BE AN ADVENTURE.
AN ADVENTURE?
OH BOY!
IN HERE! BUT DON'T TELL ANYONE!
very secret shhh!
IT'S HIDDEN!
WHAT IS IT? HAVE YOU BEEN MAKING A TOILET?
HEE HEE. NO, SILLY. IT'S A ROCKET SHIP!!
BWOOM!
BWOOM!
ARE YOU ...SURE?
SURE! YOU CAME FROM SPACE, MISTER MONKEY. WE WANNA GO UP THERE TOO!
SPLUCH!

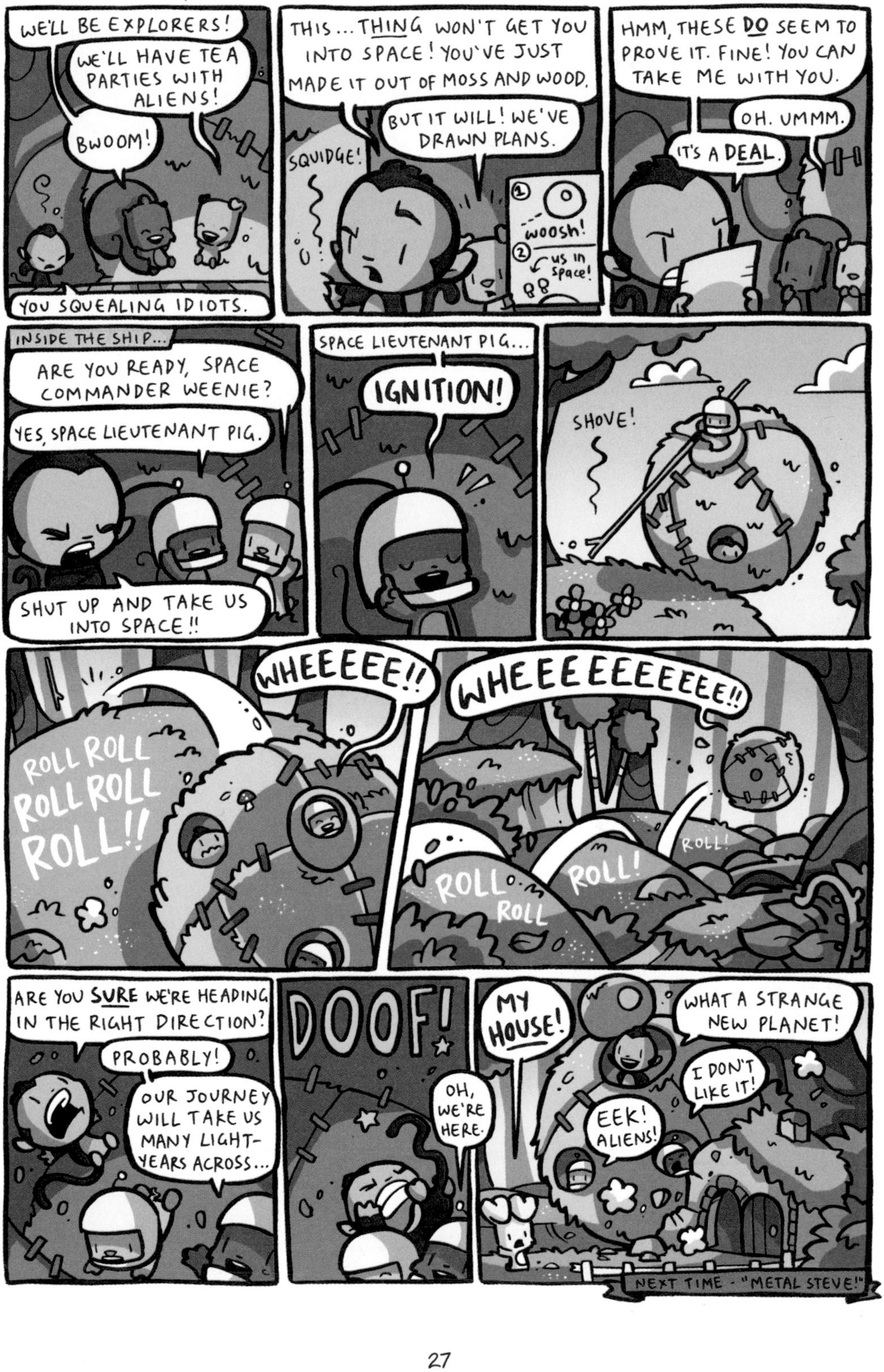

WE'LL BE EXPLORERS!
WE'LL HAVE TEA PARTIES WITH ALIENS!
BWOOM!
YOU SQUEALING IDIOTS.
THIS... THING WON'T GET YOU INTO SPACE! YOU'VE JUST MADE IT OUT OF MOSS AND WOOD.
BUT IT WILL! WE'VE DRAWN PLANS.
SQUIDGE!
1
WOOSH!
2
US IN SPACE!
HMM, THESE DO SEEM TO PROVE IT. FINE! YOU CAN TAKE ME WITH YOU.
OH. UMMM.
IT'S A DEAL.
INSIDE THE SHIP...
ARE YOU READY, SPACE COMMANDER WEENIE?
YES, SPACE LIEUTENANT PIG.
SHUT UP AND TAKE US INTO SPACE!!
SPACE LIEUTENANT PIG...
IGNITION!
SHOVE!
ROLL ROLL ROLL ROLL ROLL!!
WHEEEEE!!
WHEEEEEEEEEE!!
ROLL!
ROLL
ROLL
ROLL!
ARE YOU SURE WE'RE HEADING IN THE RIGHT DIRECTION?
PROBABLY!
OUR JOURNEY WILL TAKE US MANY LIGHT-YEARS ACROSS...
DOOF!
OH, WE'RE HERE.
MY HOUSE!
WHAT A STRANGE NEW PLANET!
I DON'T LIKE IT!
EEK! ALIENS!
NEXT TIME - "METAL STEVE!"

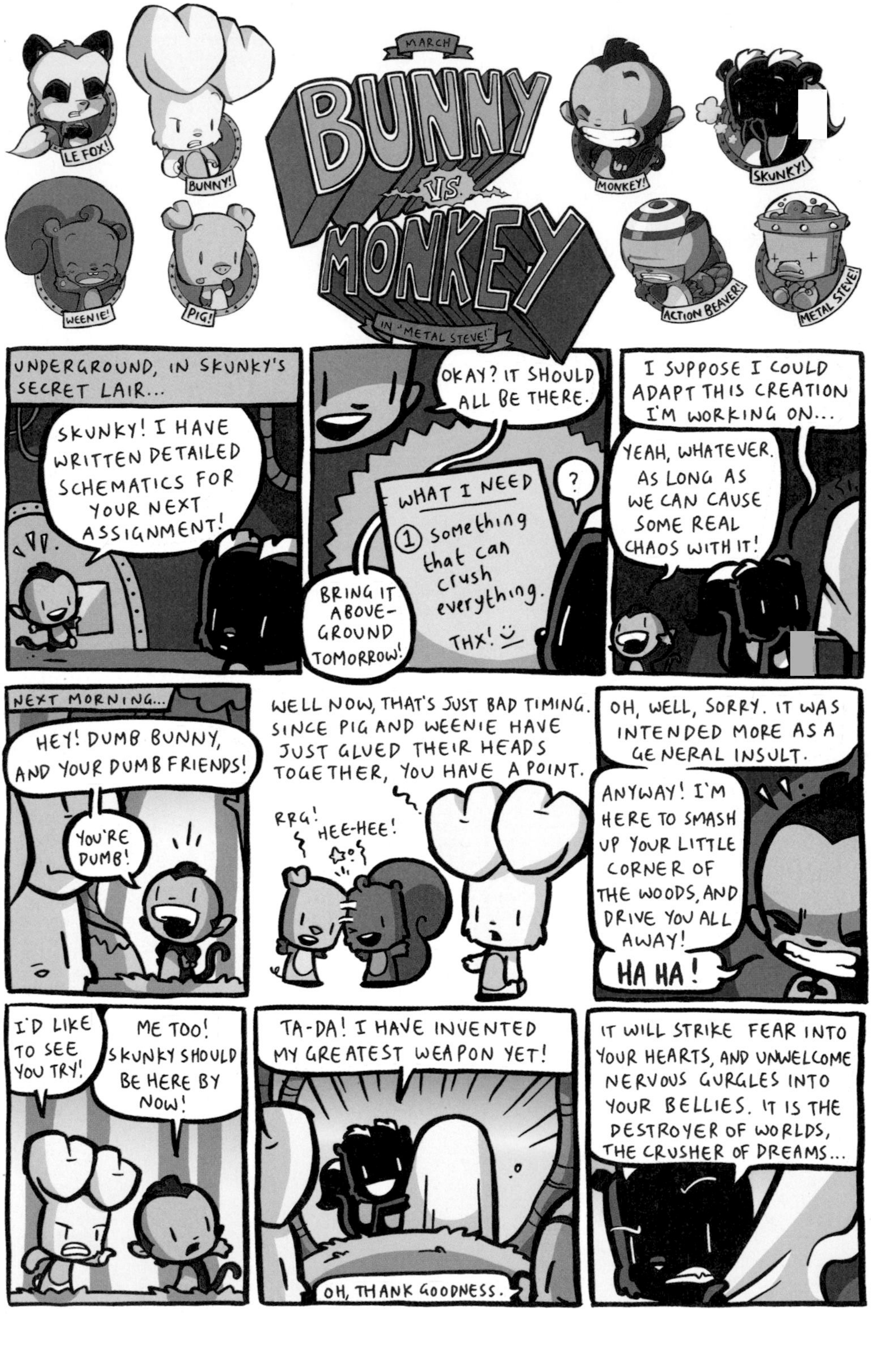

LE FOX!
BUNNY!
MARCH
BUNNY VS MONKEY
IN "METAL STEVE!"
MONKEY!
SKUNKY!
WEENIE!
PIG!
ACTION BEAVER!
METAL STEVE!
UNDERGROUND, IN SKUNKY'S SECRET LAIR...
SKUNKY! I HAVE WRITTEN DETAILED SCHEMATICS FOR YOUR NEXT ASSIGNMENT!
OKAY? IT SHOULD ALL BE THERE.
WHAT I NEED
1 something that can crush everything.
THX!
?
BRING IT ABOVE-GROUND TOMORROW!
I SUPPOSE I COULD ADAPT THIS CREATION I'M WORKING ON...
YEAH, WHATEVER. AS LONG AS WE CAN CAUSE SOME REAL CHAOS WITH IT!
NEXT MORNING...
HEY! DUMB BUNNY, AND YOUR DUMB FRIENDS!
YOU'RE DUMB!
WELL NOW, THAT'S JUST BAD TIMING. SINCE PIG AND WEENIE HAVE JUST GLUED THEIR HEADS TOGETHER, YOU HAVE A POINT.
RRG!
HEE-HEE!
OH, WELL, SORRY. IT WAS INTENDED MORE AS A GENERAL INSULT.
ANYWAY! I'M HERE TO SMASH UP YOUR LITTLE CORNER OF THE WOODS, AND DRIVE YOU ALL AWAY!
HA HA!
I'D LIKE TO SEE YOU TRY!
ME TOO! SKUNKY SHOULD BE HERE BY NOW!
TA-DA! I HAVE INVENTED MY GREATEST WEAPON YET!
OH, THANK GOODNESS.
IT WILL STRIKE FEAR INTO YOUR HEARTS, AND UNWELCOME NERVOUS GURGLES INTO YOUR BELLIES. IT IS THE DESTROYER OF WORLDS, THE CRUSHER OF DREAMS...

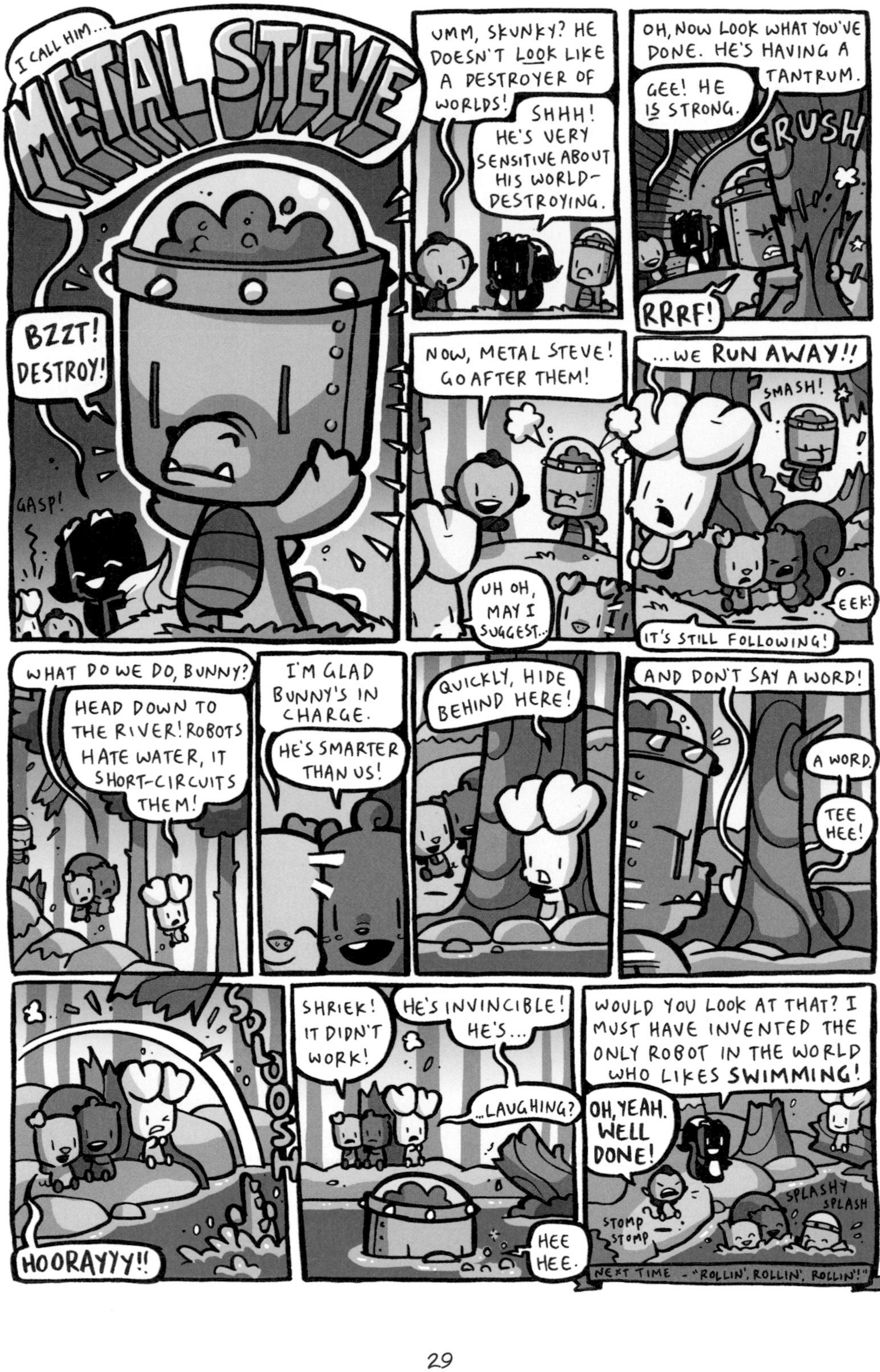
I CALL HIM...
METAL STEVE
BZZT! DESTROY!
GASP!
UMM, SKUNKY? HE DOESN'T LOOK LIKE A DESTROYER OF WORLDS!
SHHH! HE'S VERY SENSITIVE ABOUT HIS WORLD-DESTROYING.
OH, NOW LOOK WHAT YOU'VE DONE. HE'S HAVING A TANTRUM.
GEE! HE IS STRONG.
CRUSH
RRRF!
NOW, METAL STEVE! GO AFTER THEM!
UH OH, MAY I SUGGEST...
...WE RUN AWAY!!
SMASH!
EEK!
IT'S STILL FOLLOWING!
WHAT DO WE DO, BUNNY?
HEAD DOWN TO THE RIVER! ROBOTS HATE WATER, IT SHORT-CIRCUITS THEM!
I'M GLAD BUNNY'S IN CHARGE.
HE'S SMARTER THAN US!
QUICKLY, HIDE BEHIND HERE!
AND DON'T SAY A WORD!
A WORD.
TEE HEE!
SPLOOSH
HOORAYYY!!
SHRIEK! IT DIDN'T WORK!
HE'S INVINCIBLE! HE'S...
...LAUGHING?
HEE HEE.
WOULD YOU LOOK AT THAT? I MUST HAVE INVENTED THE ONLY ROBOT IN THE WORLD WHO LIKES SWIMMING!
OH, YEAH. WELL DONE!
SPLASHY SPLASH
STOMP STOMP
NEXT TIME - "ROLLIN', ROLLIN', ROLLIN'!"

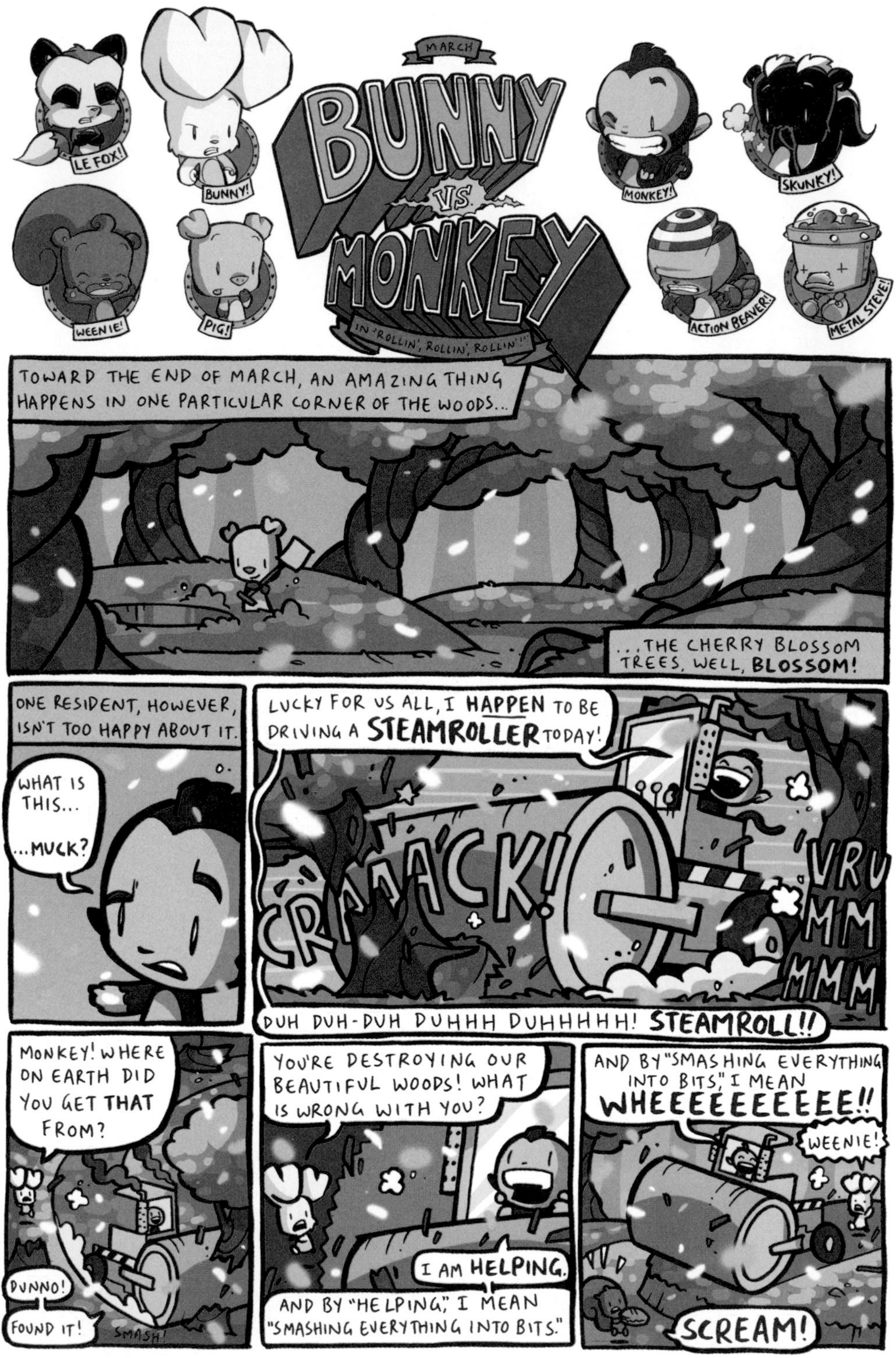

MARCH
BUNNY VS MONKEY
IN 'ROLLIN', ROLLIN', ROLLIN'!'
LE FOX!
BUNNY!
WEENIE!
PIG!
MONKEY!
SKUNKY!
ACTION BEAVER!
METAL STEVE!
TOWARD THE END OF MARCH, AN AMAZING THING HAPPENS IN ONE PARTICULAR CORNER OF THE WOODS...
...THE CHERRY BLOSSOM TREES, WELL, BLOSSOM!
ONE RESIDENT, HOWEVER, ISN'T TOO HAPPY ABOUT IT.
WHAT IS THIS...
...MUCK?
LUCKY FOR US ALL, I HAPPEN TO BE DRIVING A STEAMROLLER TODAY!
CRAAACK!
VRUMMMMMM
DUH DUH-DUH DUHHH DUHHHHH! STEAMROLL!!
MONKEY! WHERE ON EARTH DID YOU GET THAT FROM?
DUNNO!
FOUND IT!
SMASH!
YOU'RE DESTROYING OUR BEAUTIFUL WOODS! WHAT IS WRONG WITH YOU?
I AM HELPING.
AND BY "HELPING," I MEAN "SMASHING EVERYTHING INTO BITS."
AND BY "SMASHING EVERYTHING INTO BITS," I MEAN WHEEEEEEEEEE!!
WEENIE!
SCREAM!

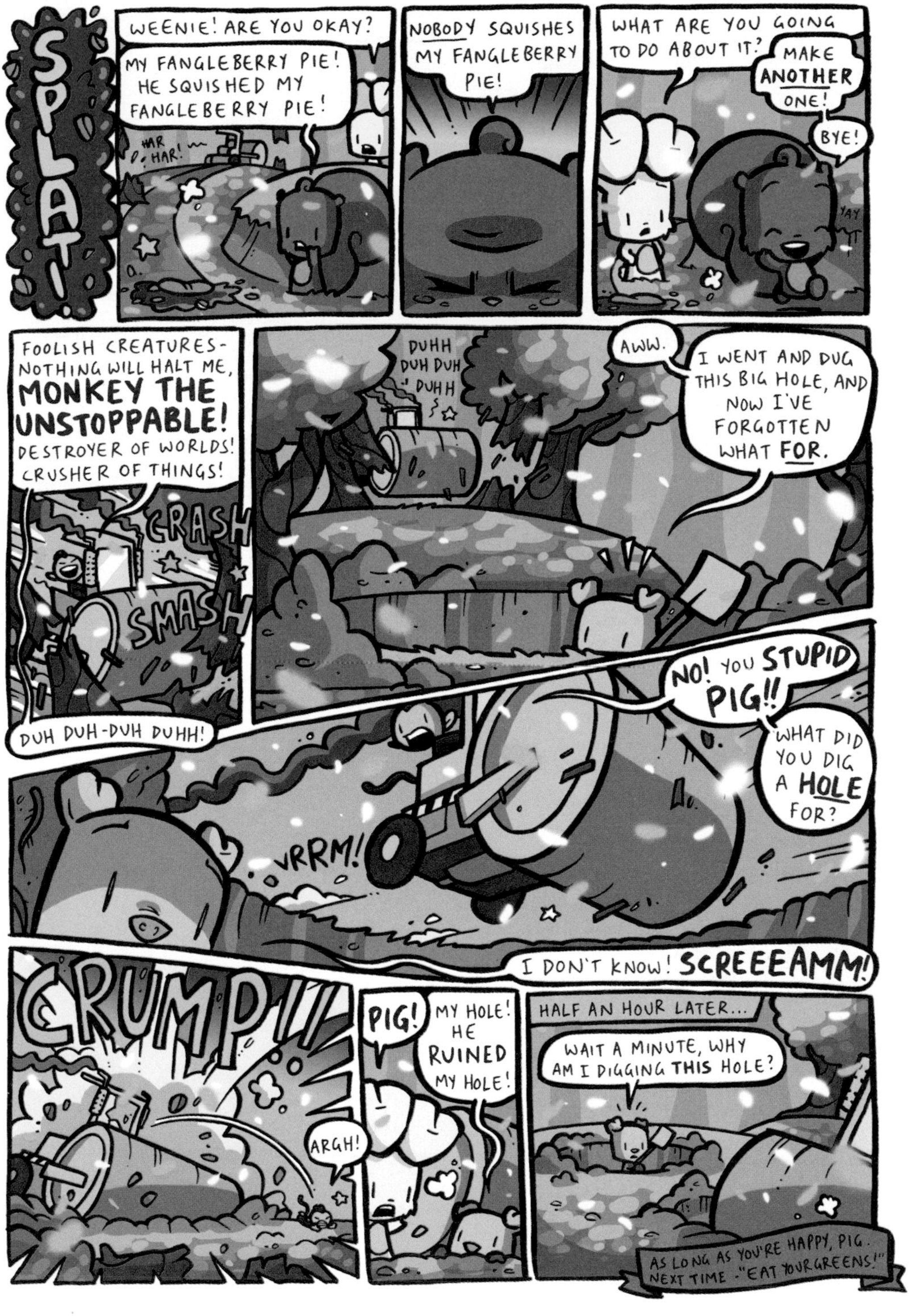
SPLAT!
WEENIE! ARE YOU OKAY?
MY FANGLEBERRY PIE! HE SQUISHED MY FANGLEBERRY PIE!
HAR HAR!
NOBODY SQUISHES MY FANGLEBERRY PIE!
WHAT ARE YOU GOING TO DO ABOUT IT?
MAKE ANOTHER ONE!
BYE!
YAY
FOOLISH CREATURES- NOTHING WILL HALT ME, MONKEY THE UNSTOPPABLE! DESTROYER OF WORLDS! CRUSHER OF THINGS!
CRASH
SMASH
DUH DUH-DUH DUHH!
DUHH DUH DUH DUHH
AWW.
I WENT AND DUG THIS BIG HOLE, AND NOW I'VE FORGOTTEN WHAT FOR.
NO! YOU STUPID PIG!!
WHAT DID YOU DIG A HOLE FOR?
VRRM!
I DON'T KNOW! SCREEEAMM!
CRUMP!!
PIG!
MY HOLE! HE RUINED MY HOLE!
ARGH!
HALF AN HOUR LATER...
WAIT A MINUTE, WHY AM I DIGGING THIS HOLE?
AS LONG AS YOU'RE HAPPY, PIG.
NEXT TIME - "EAT YOUR GREENS!"

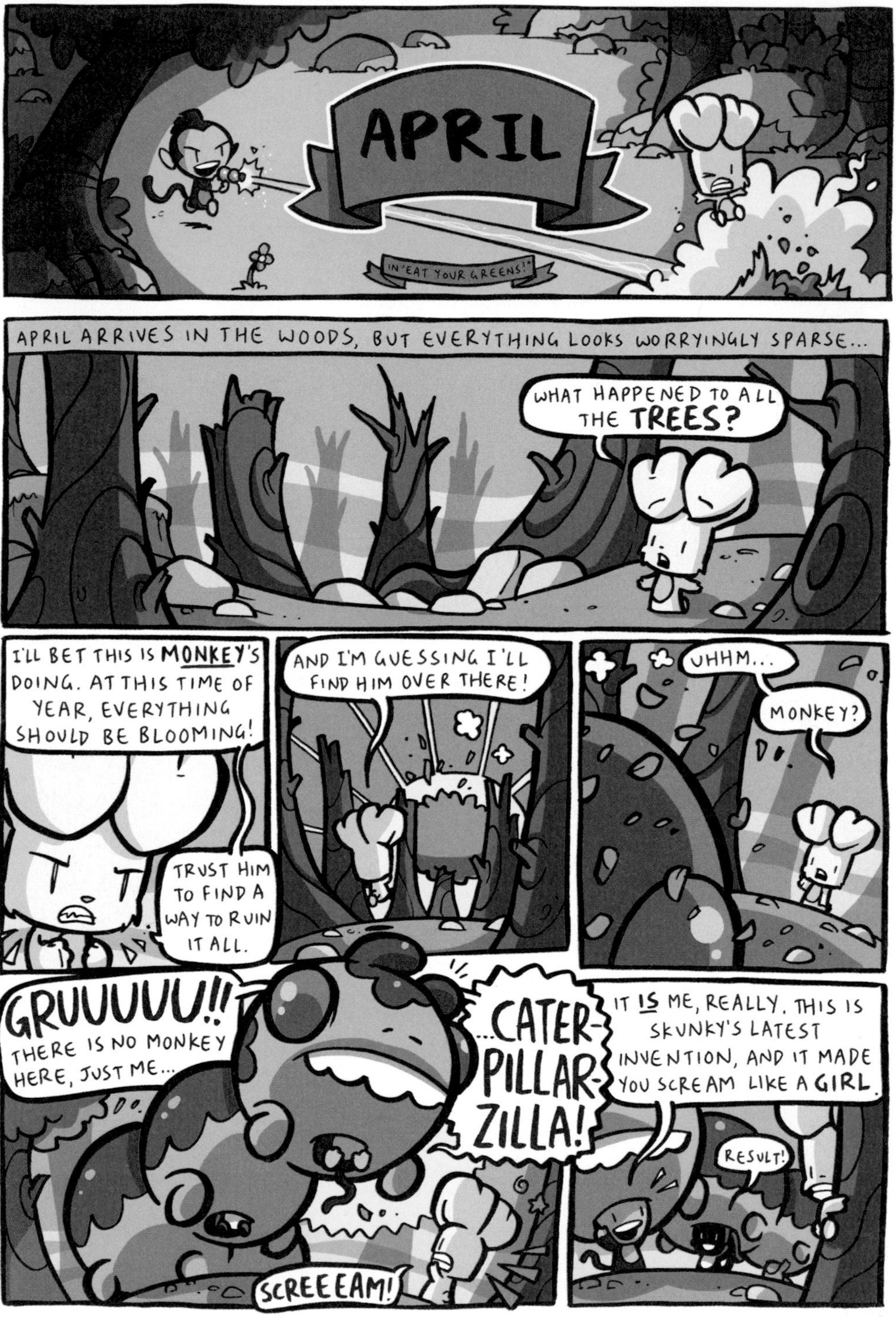
APRIL
IN "EAT YOUR GREENS!"
APRIL ARRIVES IN THE WOODS, BUT EVERYTHING LOOKS WORRYINGLY SPARSE...
WHAT HAPPENED TO ALL THE TREES?
I'LL BET THIS IS MONKEY'S DOING. AT THIS TIME OF YEAR, EVERYTHING SHOULD BE BLOOMING!
TRUST HIM TO FIND A WAY TO RUIN IT ALL.
AND I'M GUESSING I'LL FIND HIM OVER THERE!
UHHM...
MONKEY?
GRUUUUU!! THERE IS NO MONKEY HERE, JUST ME...
...CATER-PILLAR-ZILLA!
SCREEEAM!
IT IS ME, REALLY. THIS IS SKUNKY'S LATEST INVENTION, AND IT MADE YOU SCREAM LIKE A GIRL.
RESULT!

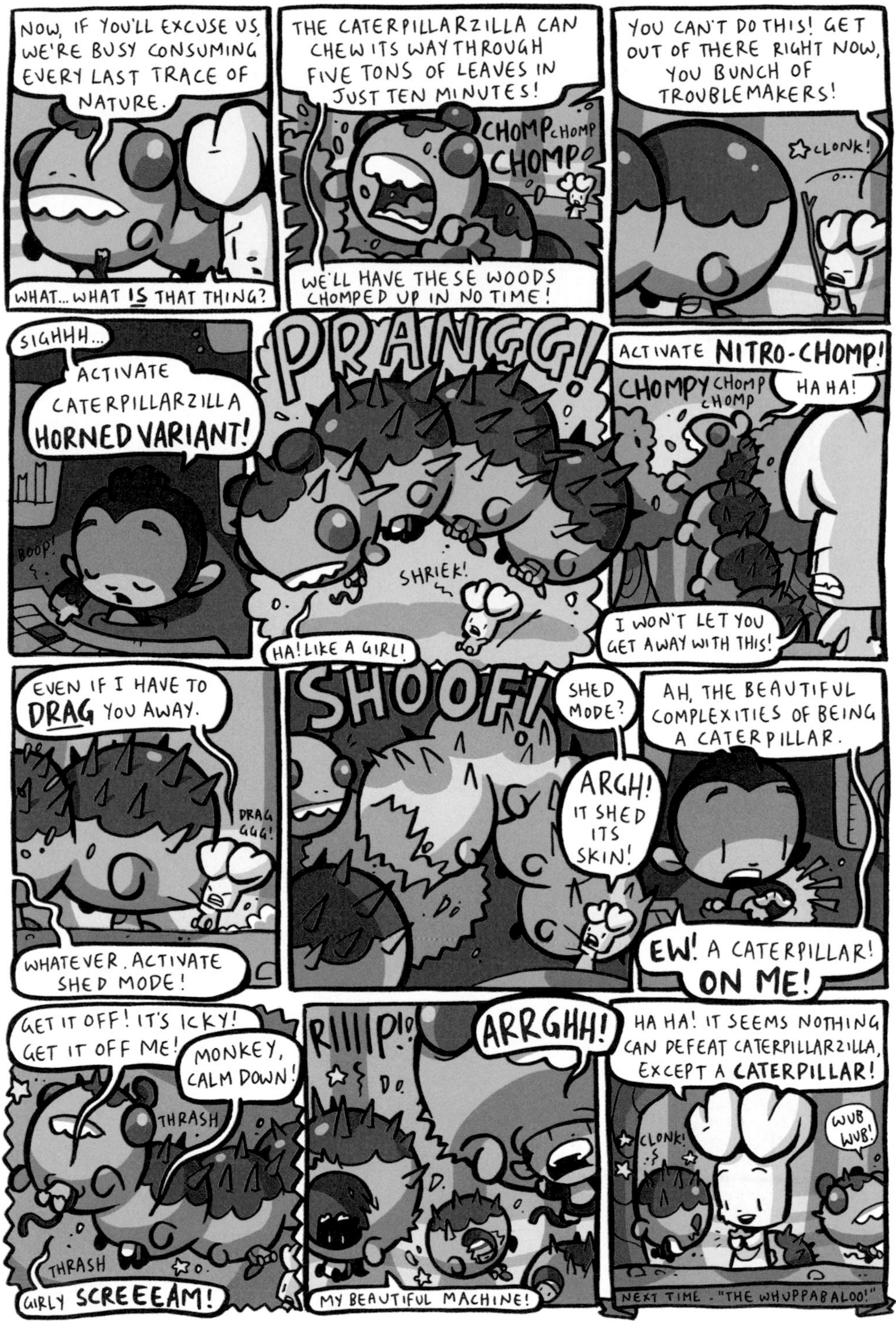
NOW, IF YOU'LL EXCUSE US, WE'RE BUSY CONSUMING EVERY LAST TRACE OF NATURE.
WHAT... WHAT IS THAT THING?
THE CATERPILLARZILLA CAN CHEW ITS WAY THROUGH FIVE TONS OF LEAVES IN JUST TEN MINUTES!
CHOMP CHOMP CHOMP
WE'LL HAVE THESE WOODS CHOMPED UP IN NO TIME!
YOU CAN'T DO THIS! GET OUT OF THERE RIGHT NOW, YOU BUNCH OF TROUBLEMAKERS!
CLONK!
SIGHHH...
ACTIVATE CATERPILLARZILLA HORNED VARIANT!
BOOP!
PRANGG!
SHRIEK!
HA! LIKE A GIRL!
ACTIVATE NITRO-CHOMP!
CHOMPY CHOMP CHOMP
HA HA!
I WON'T LET YOU GET AWAY WITH THIS!
EVEN IF I HAVE TO DRAG YOU AWAY.
DRAGGGG!
WHATEVER. ACTIVATE SHED MODE!
SHOOF!
SHED MODE?
ARGH! IT SHED ITS SKIN!
AH, THE BEAUTIFUL COMPLEXITIES OF BEING A CATERPILLAR.
EW! A CATERPILLAR! ON ME!
GET IT OFF! IT'S ICKY! GET IT OFF ME!
MONKEY, CALM DOWN!
THRASH
THRASH
GIRLY SCREEEAM!
RIIIP!
ARRGHH!
MY BEAUTIFUL MACHINE!
HA HA! IT SEEMS NOTHING CAN DEFEAT CATERPILLARZILLA, EXCEPT A CATERPILLAR!
CLONK!
WUB WUB!
NEXT TIME - "THE WHUPPABALOO!"

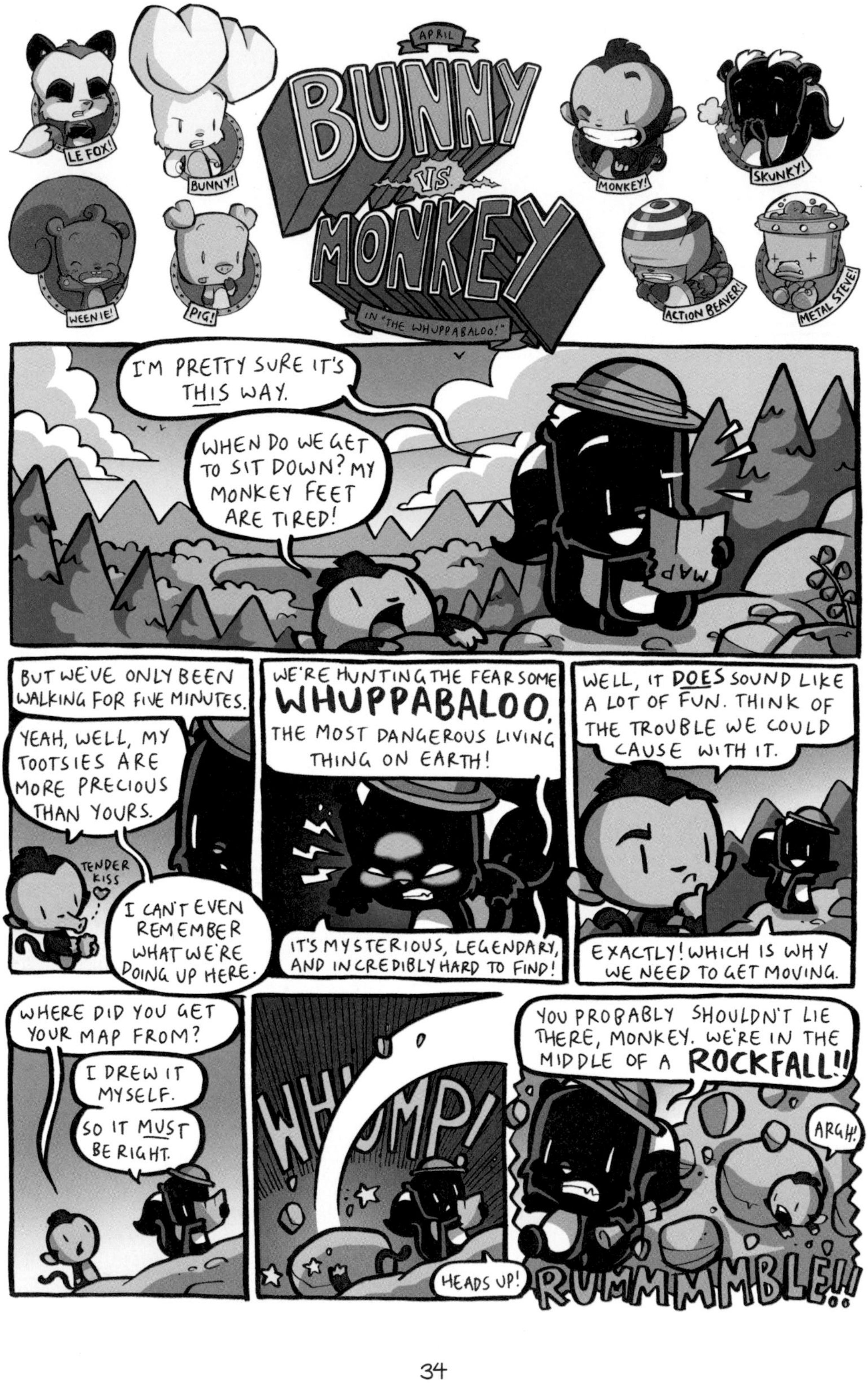
LE FOX!
BUNNY!
APRIL
BUNNY VS MONKEY
IN "THE WHUPPABALOO!"
MONKEY!
SKUNKY!
WEENIE!
PIG!
ACTION BEAVER!
METAL STEVE!
I'M PRETTY SURE IT'S THIS WAY.
WHEN DO WE GET TO SIT DOWN? MY MONKEY FEET ARE TIRED!
MAP
BUT WE'VE ONLY BEEN WALKING FOR FIVE MINUTES.
YEAH, WELL, MY TOOTSIES ARE MORE PRECIOUS THAN YOURS.
TENDER KISS
I CAN'T EVEN REMEMBER WHAT WE'RE DOING UP HERE.
WE'RE HUNTING THE FEARSOME WHUPPABALOO, THE MOST DANGEROUS LIVING THING ON EARTH!
IT'S MYSTERIOUS, LEGENDARY, AND INCREDIBLY HARD TO FIND!
WELL, IT DOES SOUND LIKE A LOT OF FUN. THINK OF THE TROUBLE WE COULD CAUSE WITH IT.
EXACTLY! WHICH IS WHY WE NEED TO GET MOVING.
WHERE DID YOU GET YOUR MAP FROM?
I DREW IT MYSELF.
SO IT MUST BE RIGHT.
WHUMP!
HEADS UP!
YOU PROBABLY SHOULDN'T LIE THERE, MONKEY. WE'RE IN THE MIDDLE OF A ROCKFALL!!
ARGH!
RUMMMMMBLE!!

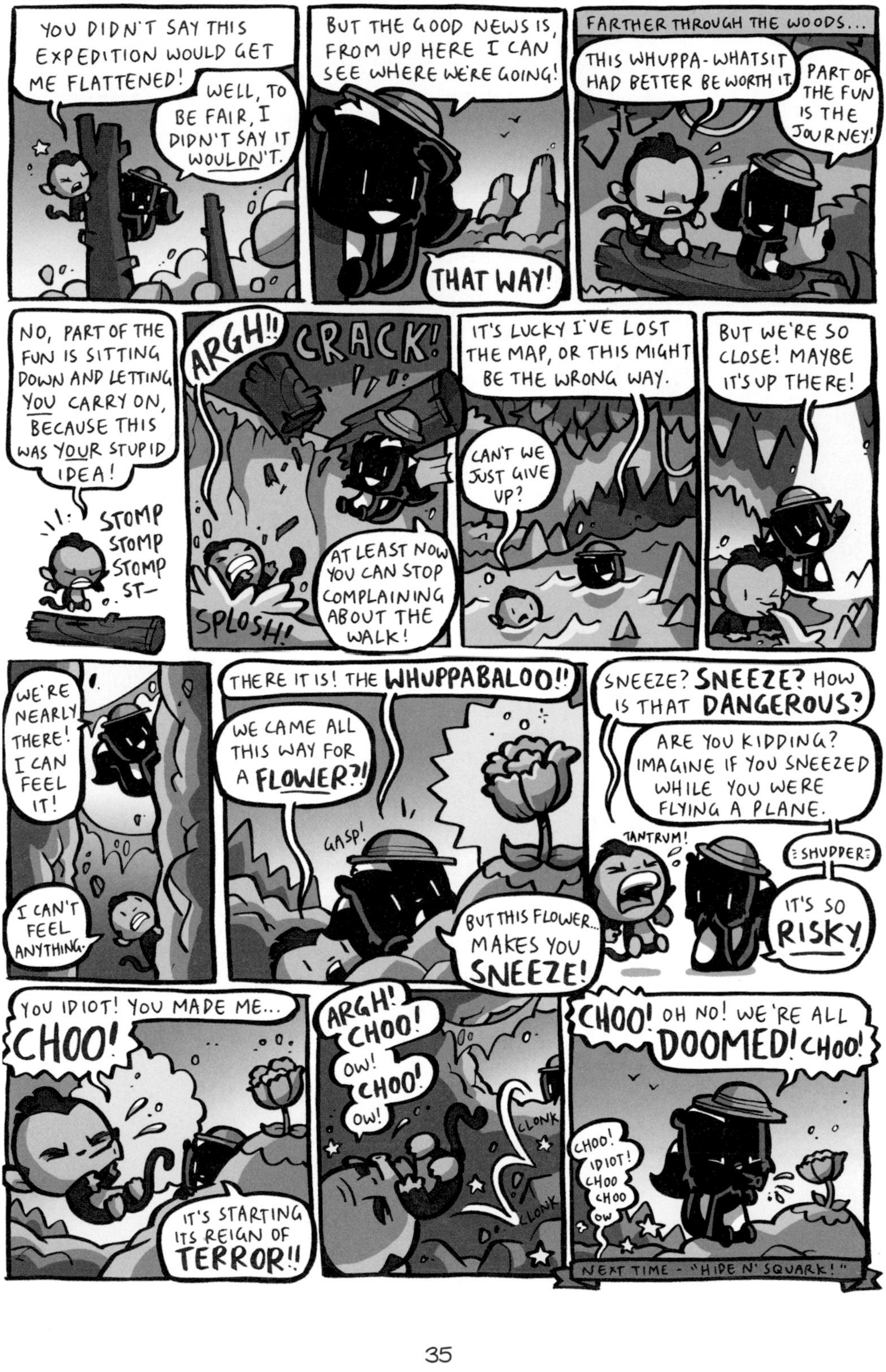
YOU DIDN'T SAY THIS EXPEDITION WOULD GET ME FLATTENED!
WELL, TO BE FAIR, I DIDN'T SAY IT WOULDN'T.
BUT THE GOOD NEWS IS, FROM UP HERE I CAN SEE WHERE WE'RE GOING!
THAT WAY!
FARTHER THROUGH THE WOODS...
THIS WHUPPA-WHATSIT HAD BETTER BE WORTH IT.
PART OF THE FUN IS THE JOURNEY!
NO, PART OF THE FUN IS SITTING DOWN AND LETTING YOU CARRY ON, BECAUSE THIS WAS YOUR STUPID IDEA!
STOMP STOMP STOMP ST—
ARGH!!
CRACK!
SPLOSH!
AT LEAST NOW YOU CAN STOP COMPLAINING ABOUT THE WALK!
IT'S LUCKY I'VE LOST THE MAP, OR THIS MIGHT BE THE WRONG WAY.
CAN'T WE JUST GIVE UP?
BUT WE'RE SO CLOSE! MAYBE IT'S UP THERE!
WE'RE NEARLY THERE! I CAN FEEL IT!
I CAN'T FEEL ANYTHING.
THERE IT IS! THE WHUPPABALOO!!
WE CAME ALL THIS WAY FOR A FLOWER?!
GASP!
BUT THIS FLOWER... MAKES YOU SNEEZE!
SNEEZE? SNEEZE? HOW IS THAT DANGEROUS?
ARE YOU KIDDING? IMAGINE IF YOU SNEEZED WHILE YOU WERE FLYING A PLANE.
TANTRUM!
SHUDDER
IT'S SO RISKY.
YOU IDIOT! YOU MADE ME... CHOO!
IT'S STARTING ITS REIGN OF TERROR!!
ARGH! CHOO! OW! CHOO! OW!
CLONK
CLONK
CHOO! OH NO! WE'RE ALL DOOMED! CHOO!
CHOO! IDIOT! CHOO CHOO OW
NEXT TIME - "HIDE N' SQUARK!"

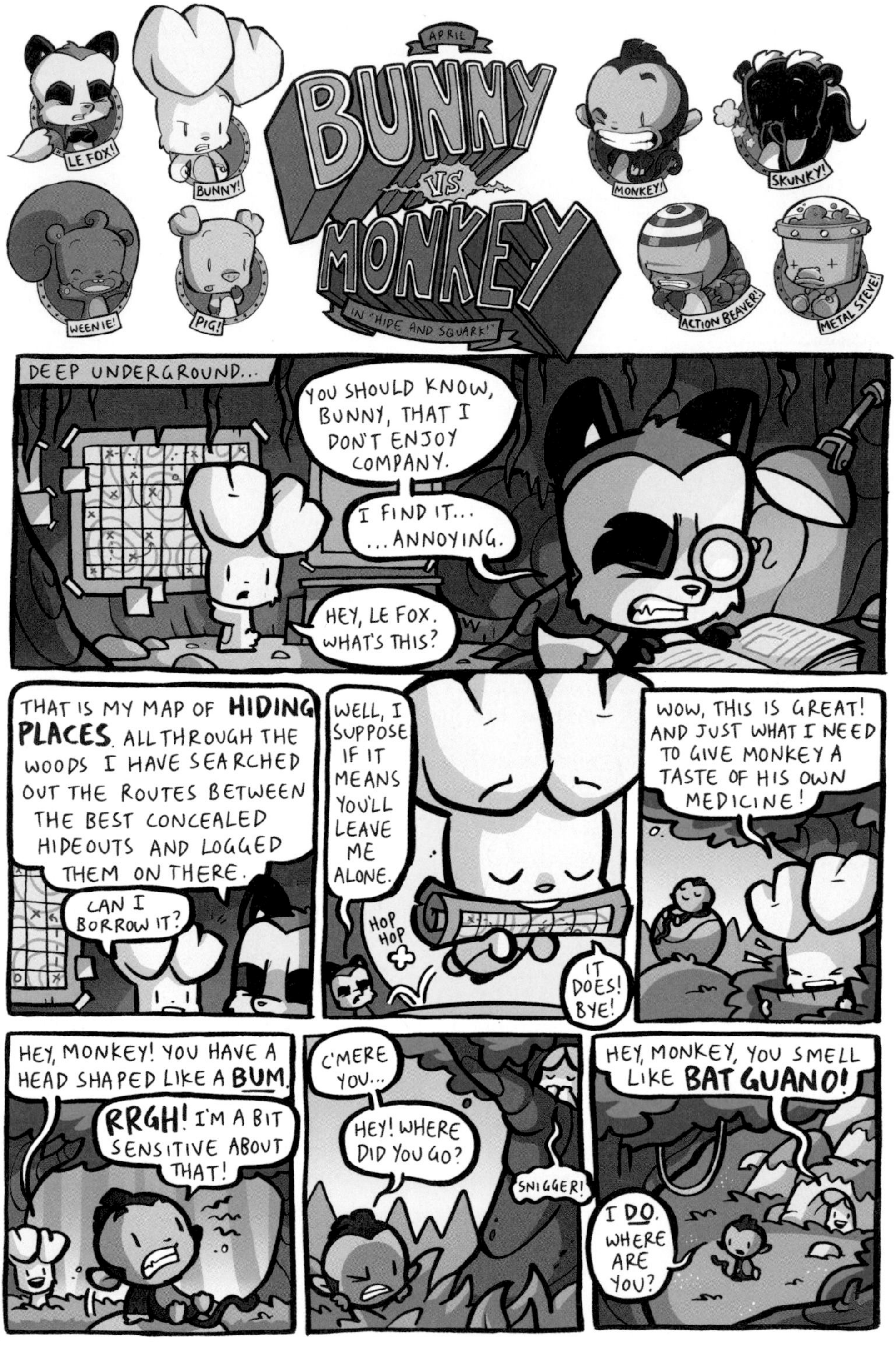

LE FOX!
BUNNY!
WEENIE!
PIG!
APRIL
BUNNY VS. MONKEY
IN "HIDE AND SQUARK!"
MONKEY!
SKUNKY!
ACTION BEAVER!
METAL STEVE!
DEEP UNDERGROUND...
YOU SHOULD KNOW, BUNNY, THAT I DON'T ENJOY COMPANY.
I FIND IT... ...ANNOYING.
HEY, LE FOX. WHAT'S THIS?
THAT IS MY MAP OF HIDING PLACES. ALL THROUGH THE WOODS I HAVE SEARCHED OUT THE ROUTES BETWEEN THE BEST CONCEALED HIDEOUTS AND LOGGED THEM ON THERE.
CAN I BORROW IT?
WELL, I SUPPOSE IF IT MEANS YOU'LL LEAVE ME ALONE.
HOP HOP
IT DOES! BYE!
WOW, THIS IS GREAT! AND JUST WHAT I NEED TO GIVE MONKEY A TASTE OF HIS OWN MEDICINE!
HEY, MONKEY! YOU HAVE A HEAD SHAPED LIKE A BUM.
RRGH! I'M A BIT SENSITIVE ABOUT THAT!
C'MERE YOU...
HEY! WHERE DID YOU GO?
SNIGGER!
HEY, MONKEY, YOU SMELL LIKE BAT GUANO!
I DO. WHERE ARE YOU?

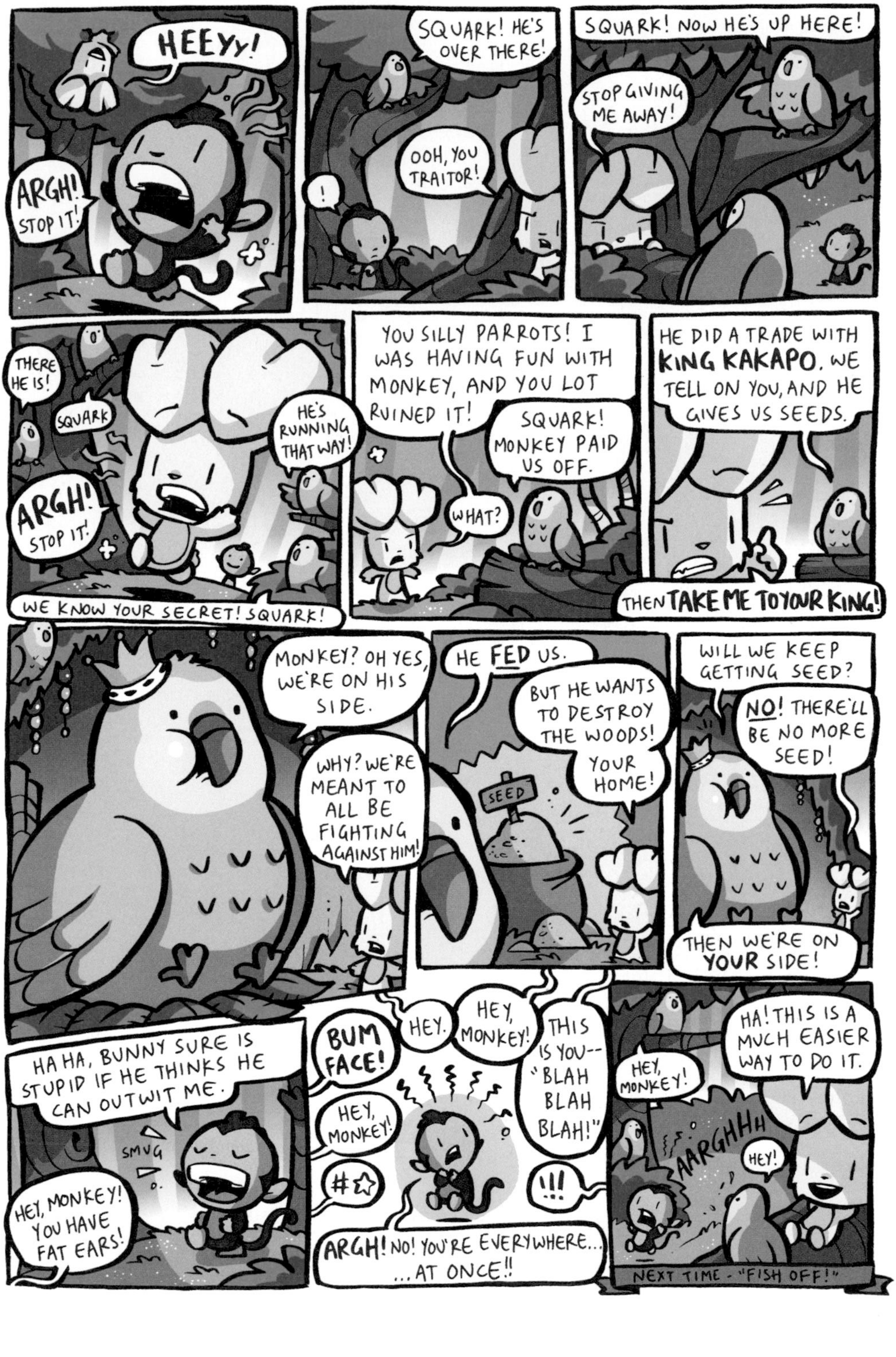
HEEYy!
ARGH! STOP IT!
SQUARK! HE'S OVER THERE!
!
OOH, YOU TRAITOR!
SQUARK! NOW HE'S UP HERE!
STOP GIVING ME AWAY!
THERE HE IS!
SQUARK
ARGH! STOP IT!
HE'S RUNNING THAT WAY!
WE KNOW YOUR SECRET! SQUARK!
YOU SILLY PARROTS! I WAS HAVING FUN WITH MONKEY, AND YOU LOT RUINED IT!
SQUARK! MONKEY PAID US OFF.
WHAT?
HE DID A TRADE WITH KING KAKAPO. WE TELL ON YOU, AND HE GIVES US SEEDS.
THEN TAKE ME TO YOUR KING!
MONKEY? OH YES, WE'RE ON HIS SIDE.
WHY? WE'RE MEANT TO ALL BE FIGHTING AGAINST HIM!
HE FED US.
BUT HE WANTS TO DESTROY THE WOODS! YOUR HOME!
SEED
WILL WE KEEP GETTING SEED?
NO! THERE'LL BE NO MORE SEED!
THEN WE'RE ON YOUR SIDE!
HA HA, BUNNY SURE IS STUPID IF HE THINKS HE CAN OUTWIT ME.
SMUG
HEY, MONKEY! YOU HAVE FAT EARS!
BUM FACE!
HEY.
HEY, MONKEY!
THIS IS YOU-- "BLAH BLAH BLAH!"
HEY, MONKEY!
#☆
!!!
ARGH! NO! YOU'RE EVERYWHERE... ...AT ONCE!!
HEY, MONKEY!
HA! THIS IS A MUCH EASIER WAY TO DO IT.
AARGHHH
HEY!
NEXT TIME - "FISH OFF!"

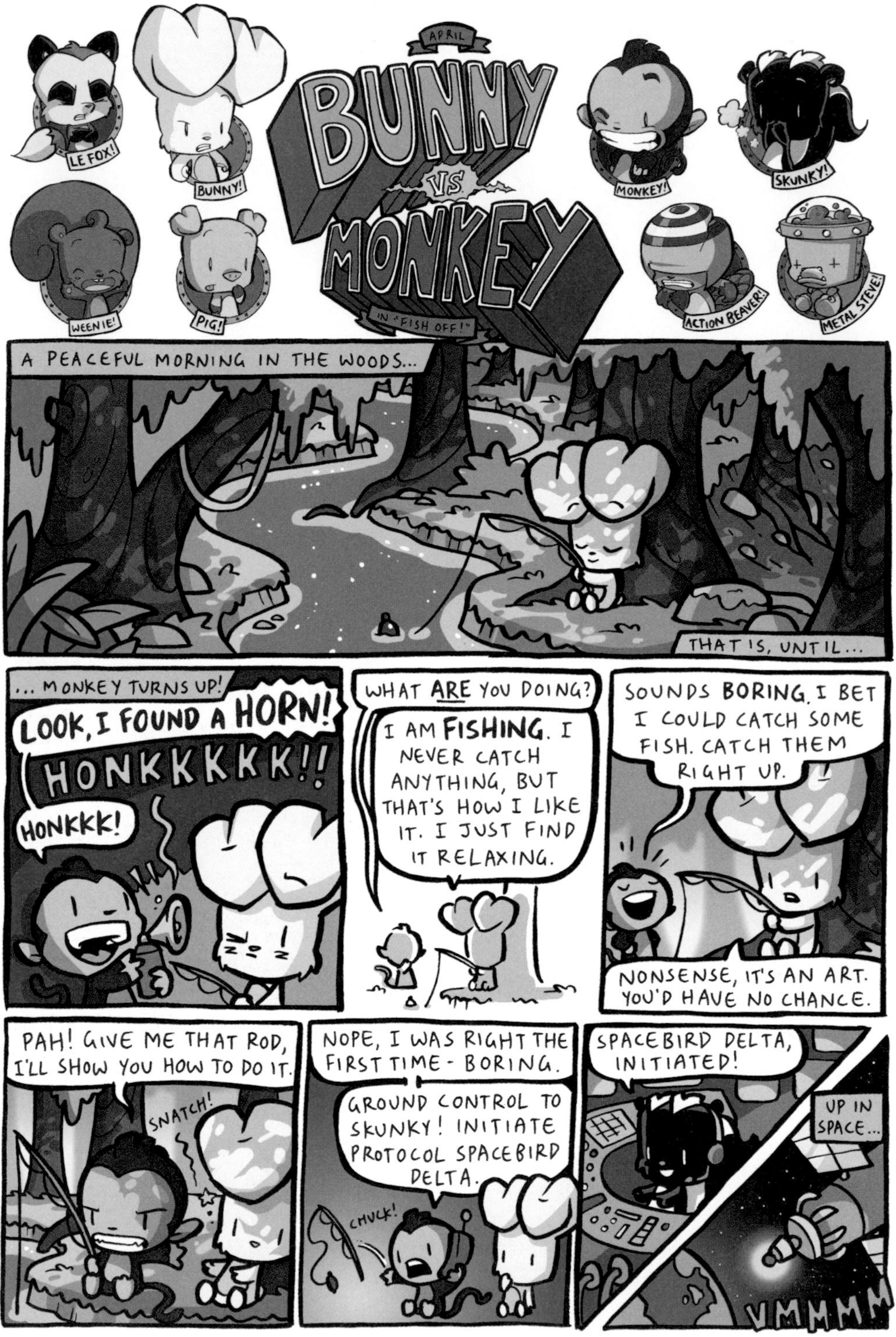

LE FOX!
BUNNY!
APRIL
BUNNY VS MONKEY
IN "FISH OFF!"
MONKEY!
SKUNKY!
WEENIE!
PIG!
ACTION BEAVER!
METAL STEVE!
A PEACEFUL MORNING IN THE WOODS...
THAT IS, UNTIL...
... MONKEY TURNS UP!
LOOK, I FOUND A HORN!
HONKKKKK!!
HONKKK!
WHAT ARE YOU DOING?
I AM FISHING. I NEVER CATCH ANYTHING, BUT THAT'S HOW I LIKE IT. I JUST FIND IT RELAXING.
SOUNDS BORING. I BET I COULD CATCH SOME FISH. CATCH THEM RIGHT UP.
NONSENSE, IT'S AN ART. YOU'D HAVE NO CHANCE.
PAH! GIVE ME THAT ROD, I'LL SHOW YOU HOW TO DO IT.
SNATCH!
NOPE, I WAS RIGHT THE FIRST TIME - BORING.
GROUND CONTROL TO SKUNKY! INITIATE PROTOCOL SPACEBIRD DELTA.
CHUCK!
SPACEBIRD DELTA, INITIATED!
UP IN SPACE...
VMMMM

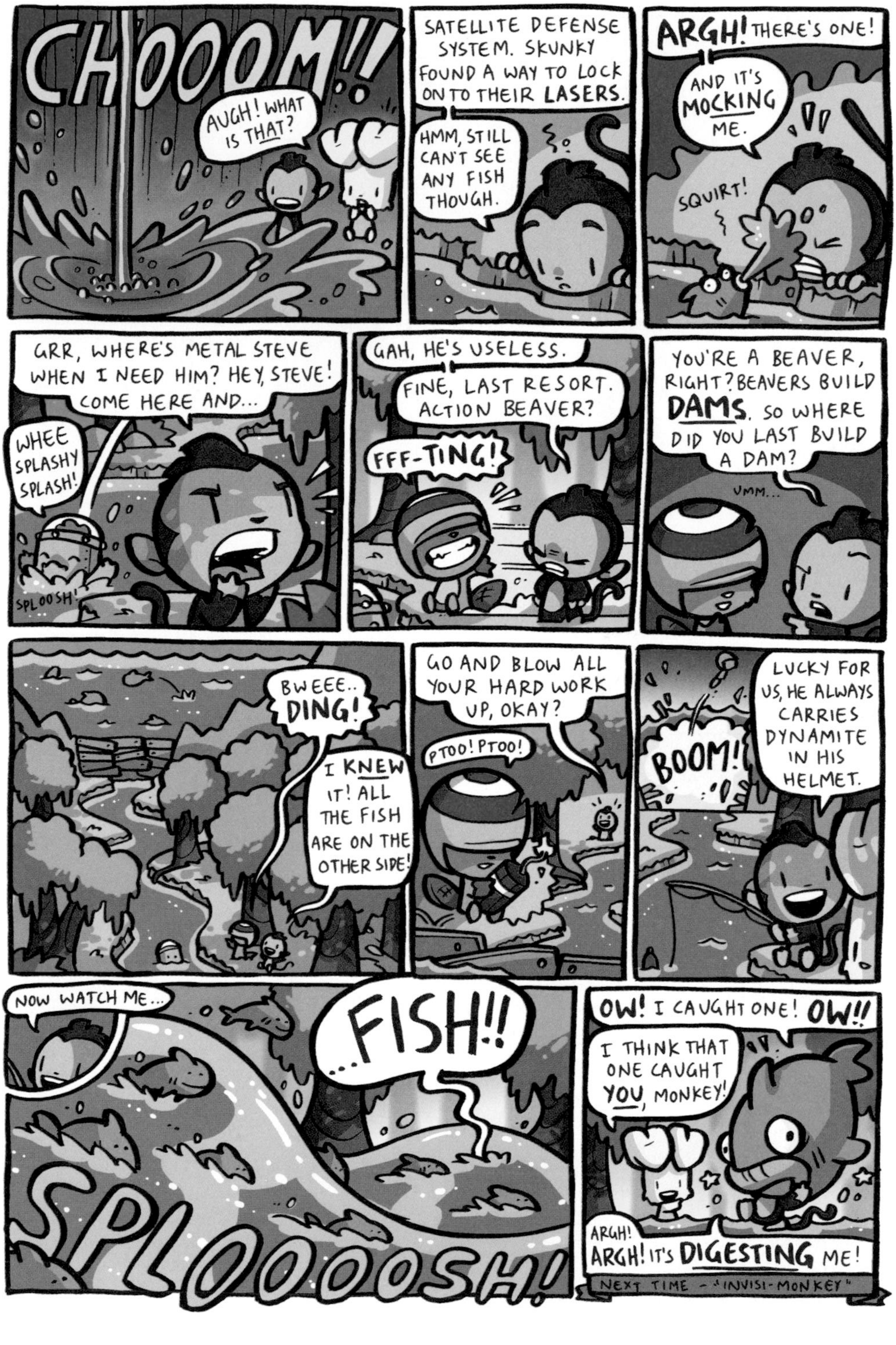
CHOOOM!!
AUGH! WHAT IS THAT?
SATELLITE DEFENSE SYSTEM. SKUNKY FOUND A WAY TO LOCK ON TO THEIR LASERS.
HMM, STILL CAN'T SEE ANY FISH THOUGH.
ARGH! THERE'S ONE!
AND IT'S MOCKING ME.
SQUIRT!
GRR, WHERE'S METAL STEVE WHEN I NEED HIM? HEY, STEVE! COME HERE AND...
WHEE SPLASHY SPLASH!
SPLOOSH!
GAH, HE'S USELESS.
FINE, LAST RESORT. ACTION BEAVER?
FFF-TING!
YOU'RE A BEAVER, RIGHT? BEAVERS BUILD DAMS. SO WHERE DID YOU LAST BUILD A DAM?
UMM...
BWEEE.. DING!
I KNEW IT! ALL THE FISH ARE ON THE OTHER SIDE!
GO AND BLOW ALL YOUR HARD WORK UP, OKAY?
PTOO! PTOO!
BOOM!
LUCKY FOR US, HE ALWAYS CARRIES DYNAMITE IN HIS HELMET.
NOW WATCH ME...
...FISH!!
SPLOOOOSH!
OW! I CAUGHT ONE! OW!!
I THINK THAT ONE CAUGHT YOU, MONKEY!
ARGH! ARGH! IT'S DIGESTING ME!
NEXT TIME - "INVISI-MONKEY"

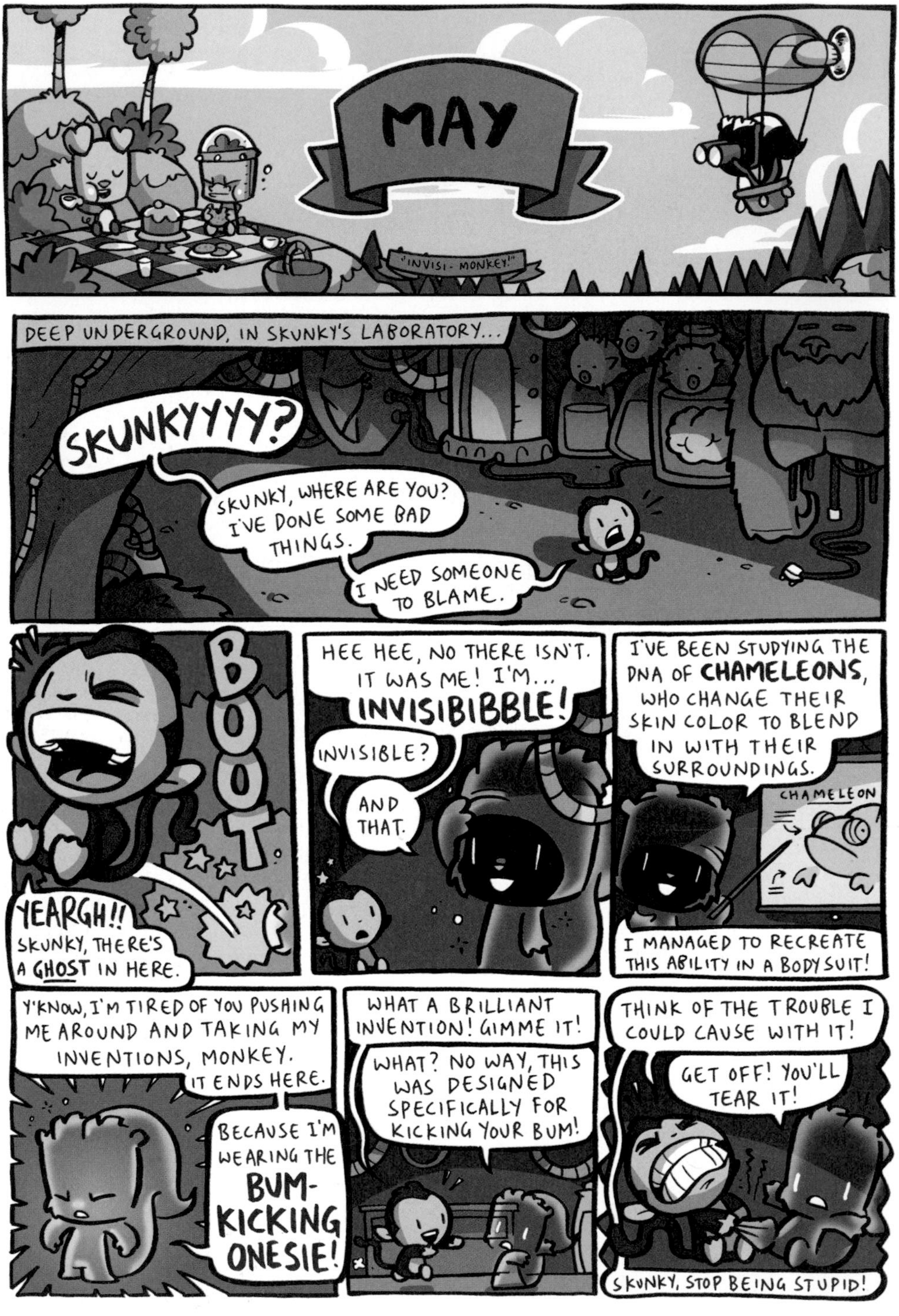
MAY
"INVISI-MONKEY!"
DEEP UNDERGROUND, IN SKUNKY'S LABORATORY...
SKUNKYYYY?
SKUNKY, WHERE ARE YOU? I'VE DONE SOME BAD THINGS.
I NEED SOMEONE TO BLAME.
BOOOT
YEARGH!! SKUNKY, THERE'S A GHOST IN HERE.
HEE HEE, NO THERE ISN'T. IT WAS ME! I'M... INVISIBIBBLE!
INVISIBLE?
AND THAT.
I'VE BEEN STUDYING THE DNA OF CHAMELEONS, WHO CHANGE THEIR SKIN COLOR TO BLEND IN WITH THEIR SURROUNDINGS.
CHAMELEON
I MANAGED TO RECREATE THIS ABILITY IN A BODYSUIT!
Y'KNOW, I'M TIRED OF YOU PUSHING ME AROUND AND TAKING MY INVENTIONS, MONKEY.
IT ENDS HERE.
BECAUSE I'M WEARING THE BUM-KICKING ONESIE!
WHAT A BRILLIANT INVENTION! GIMME IT!
WHAT? NO WAY, THIS WAS DESIGNED SPECIFICALLY FOR KICKING YOUR BUM!
THINK OF THE TROUBLE I COULD CAUSE WITH IT!
GET OFF! YOU'LL TEAR IT!
SKUNKY, STOP BEING STUPID!

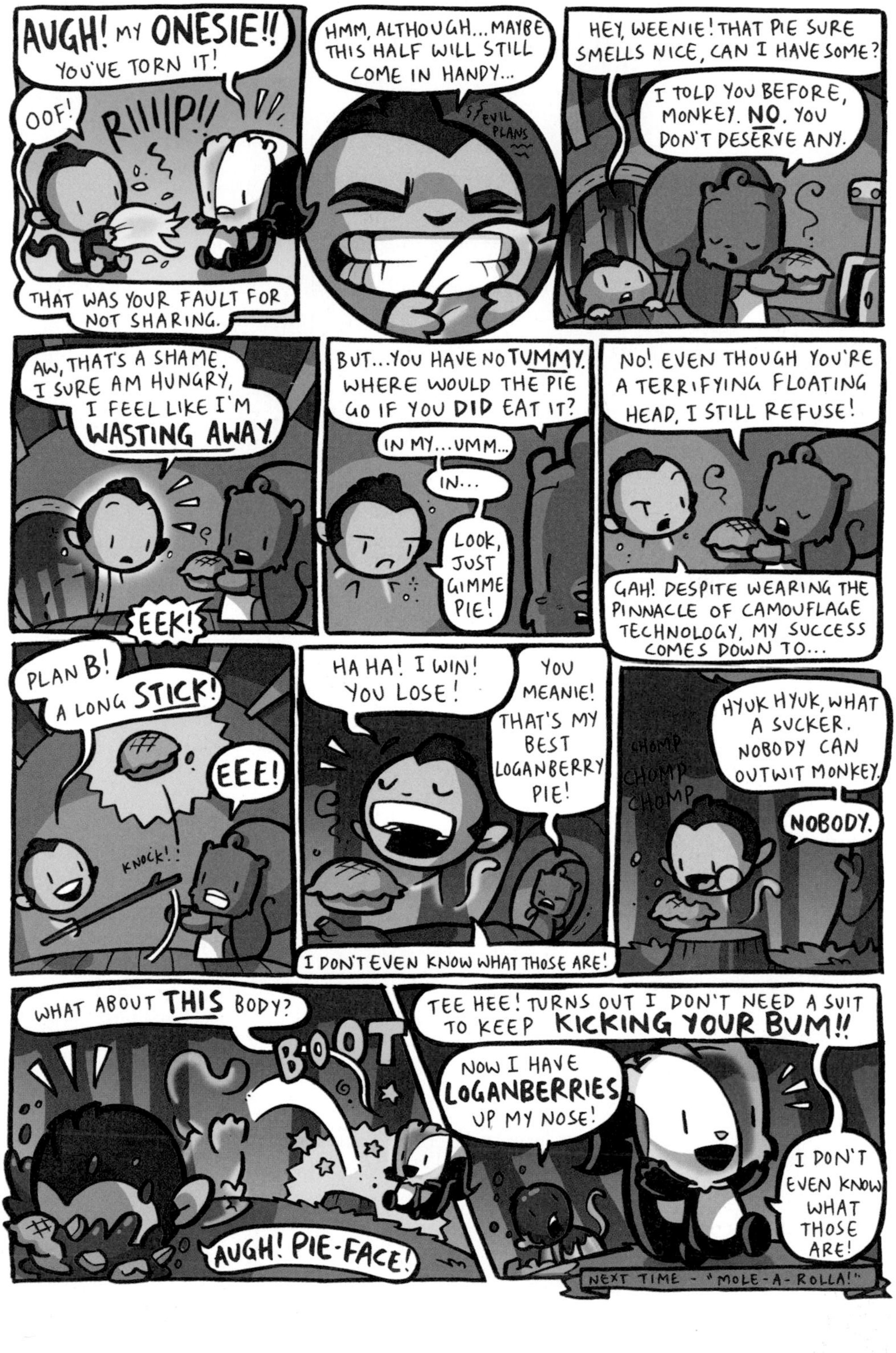

AUGH! MY ONESIE!! YOU'VE TORN IT!
OOF!
RIIIIP!!
THAT WAS YOUR FAULT FOR NOT SHARING.
HMM, ALTHOUGH... MAYBE THIS HALF WILL STILL COME IN HANDY...
EVIL PLANS
HEY, WEENIE! THAT PIE SURE SMELLS NICE, CAN I HAVE SOME?
I TOLD YOU BEFORE, MONKEY. NO. YOU DON'T DESERVE ANY.
AW, THAT'S A SHAME. I SURE AM HUNGRY, I FEEL LIKE I'M WASTING AWAY.
EEK!
BUT... YOU HAVE NO TUMMY. WHERE WOULD THE PIE GO IF YOU DID EAT IT?
IN MY... UMM...
IN...
LOOK, JUST GIMME PIE!
NO! EVEN THOUGH YOU'RE A TERRIFYING FLOATING HEAD, I STILL REFUSE!
GAH! DESPITE WEARING THE PINNACLE OF CAMOUFLAGE TECHNOLOGY, MY SUCCESS COMES DOWN TO...
PLAN B! A LONG STICK!
EEE!
KNOCK!
HA HA! I WIN! YOU LOSE!
YOU MEANIE! THAT'S MY BEST LOGANBERRY PIE!
I DON'T EVEN KNOW WHAT THOSE ARE!
CHOMP CHOMP CHOMP
HYUK HYUK, WHAT A SUCKER. NOBODY CAN OUTWIT MONKEY.
NOBODY.
WHAT ABOUT THIS BODY?
BOOT
AUGH! PIE-FACE!
TEE HEE! TURNS OUT I DON'T NEED A SUIT TO KEEP KICKING YOUR BUM!!
NOW I HAVE LOGANBERRIES UP MY NOSE!
I DON'T EVEN KNOW WHAT THOSE ARE!
NEXT TIME - "MOLE-A-ROLLA!"

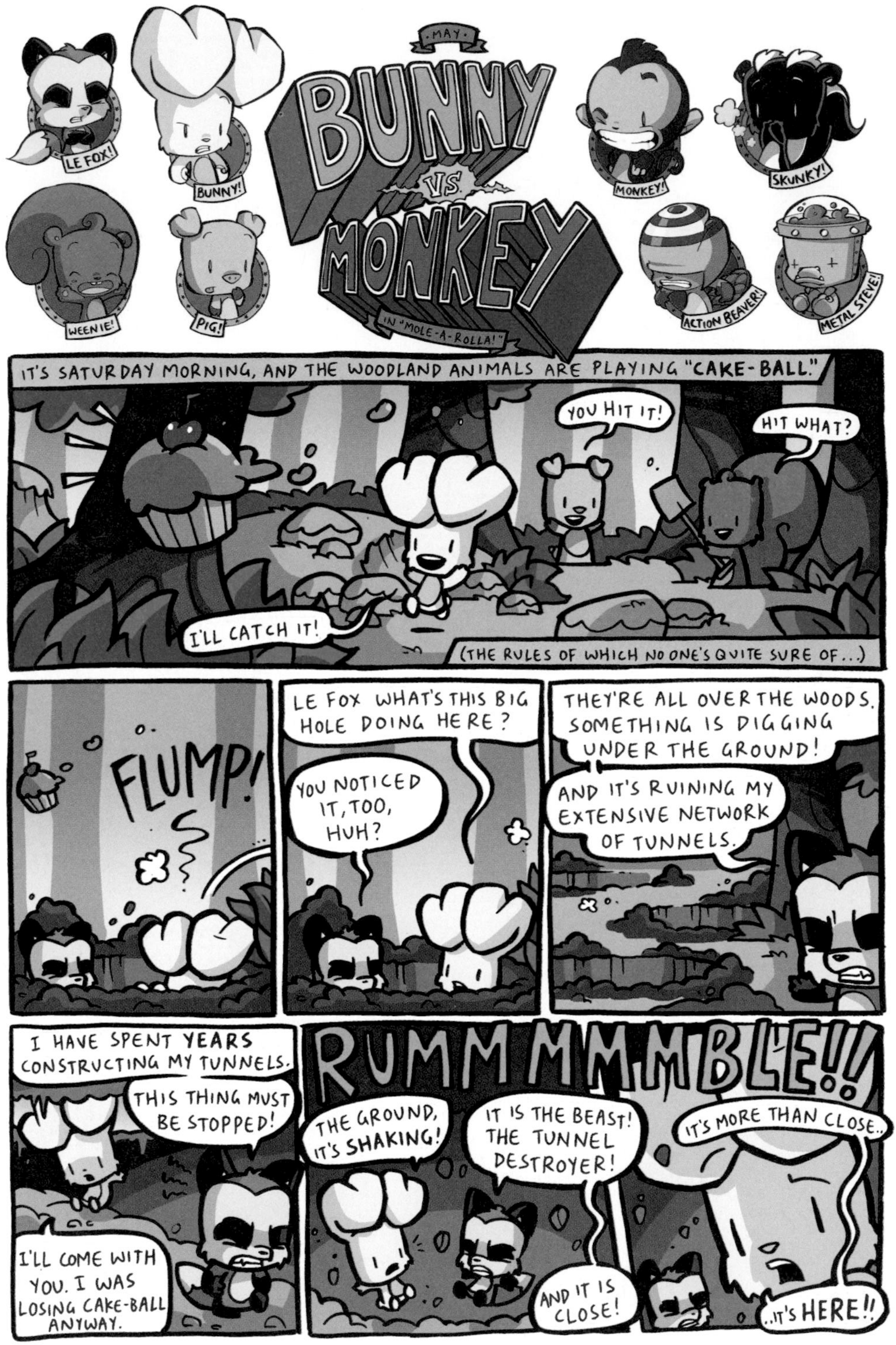
LE FOX!
BUNNY!
WEENIE!
PIG!
MAY
BUNNY VS MONKEY
IN "MOLE-A-ROLLA!"
MONKEY!
SKUNKY!
ACTION BEAVER!
METAL STEVE!
IT'S SATURDAY MORNING, AND THE WOODLAND ANIMALS ARE PLAYING "CAKE-BALL."
YOU HIT IT!
HIT WHAT?
I'LL CATCH IT!
(THE RULES OF WHICH NO ONE'S QUITE SURE OF...)
FLUMP!
LE FOX WHAT'S THIS BIG HOLE DOING HERE?
YOU NOTICED IT, TOO, HUH?
THEY'RE ALL OVER THE WOODS. SOMETHING IS DIGGING UNDER THE GROUND!
AND IT'S RUINING MY EXTENSIVE NETWORK OF TUNNELS.
I HAVE SPENT YEARS CONSTRUCTING MY TUNNELS.
THIS THING MUST BE STOPPED!
I'LL COME WITH YOU. I WAS LOSING CAKE-BALL ANYWAY.
RUMMMMMMBLE!!!
THE GROUND, IT'S SHAKING!
IT IS THE BEAST! THE TUNNEL DESTROYER!
AND IT IS CLOSE!
IT'S MORE THAN CLOSE..
..IT'S HERE!!

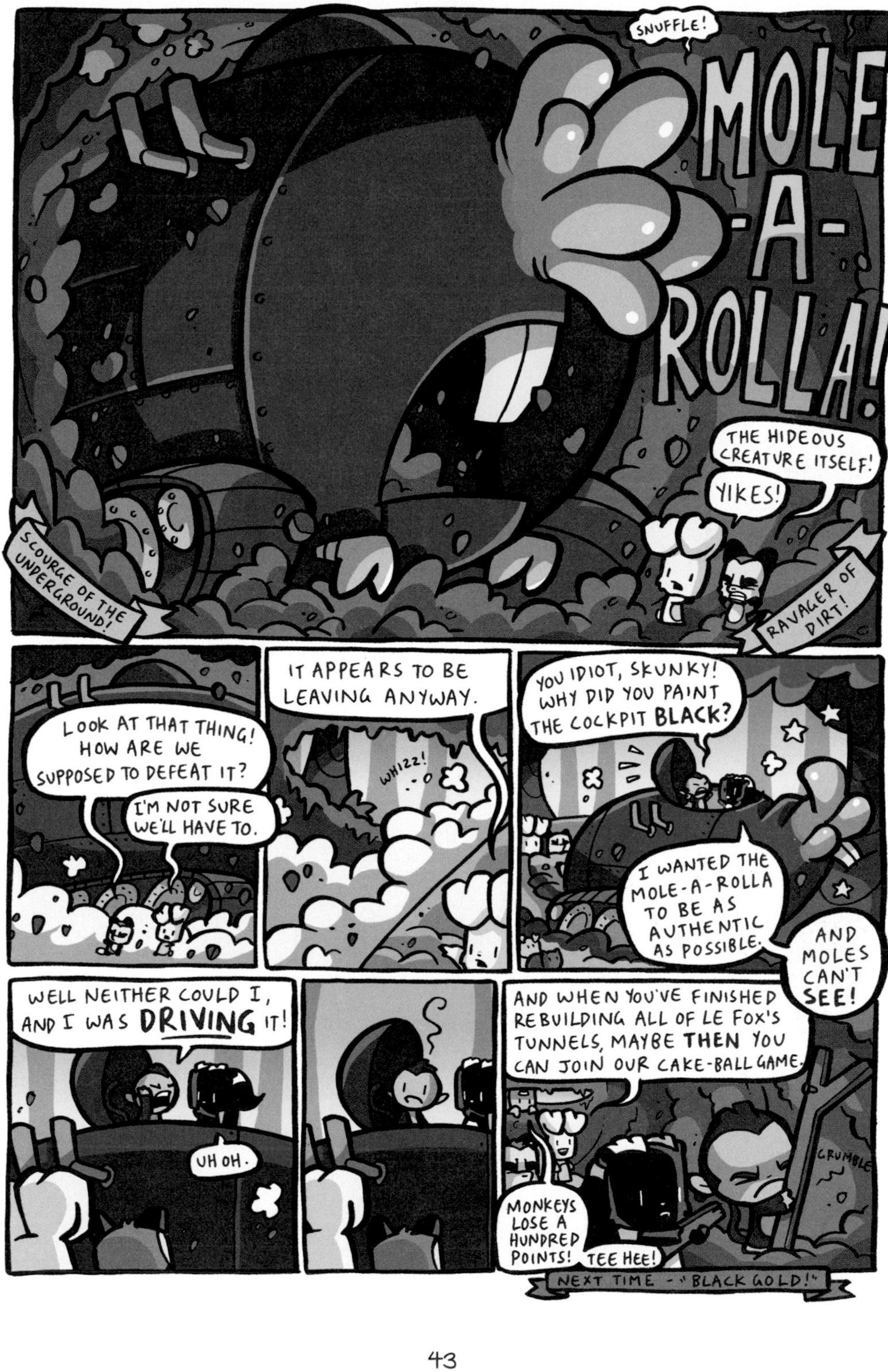
SNUFFLE!
MOLE-A-ROLLA!
THE HIDEOUS CREATURE ITSELF!
YIKES!
SCOURGE OF THE UNDERGROUND!
RAVAGER OF DIRT!
LOOK AT THAT THING! HOW ARE WE SUPPOSED TO DEFEAT IT?
I'M NOT SURE WE'LL HAVE TO.
IT APPEARS TO BE LEAVING ANYWAY.
WHIZZ!
YOU IDIOT, SKUNKY! WHY DID YOU PAINT THE COCKPIT BLACK?
I WANTED THE MOLE-A-ROLLA TO BE AS AUTHENTIC AS POSSIBLE.
AND MOLES CAN'T SEE!
WELL NEITHER COULD I, AND I WAS DRIVING IT!
UH OH.
AND WHEN YOU'VE FINISHED REBUILDING ALL OF LE FOX'S TUNNELS, MAYBE THEN YOU CAN JOIN OUR CAKE-BALL GAME.
CRUMBLE
MONKEYS LOSE A HUNDRED POINTS!
TEE HEE!
NEXT TIME - "BLACK GOLD!"

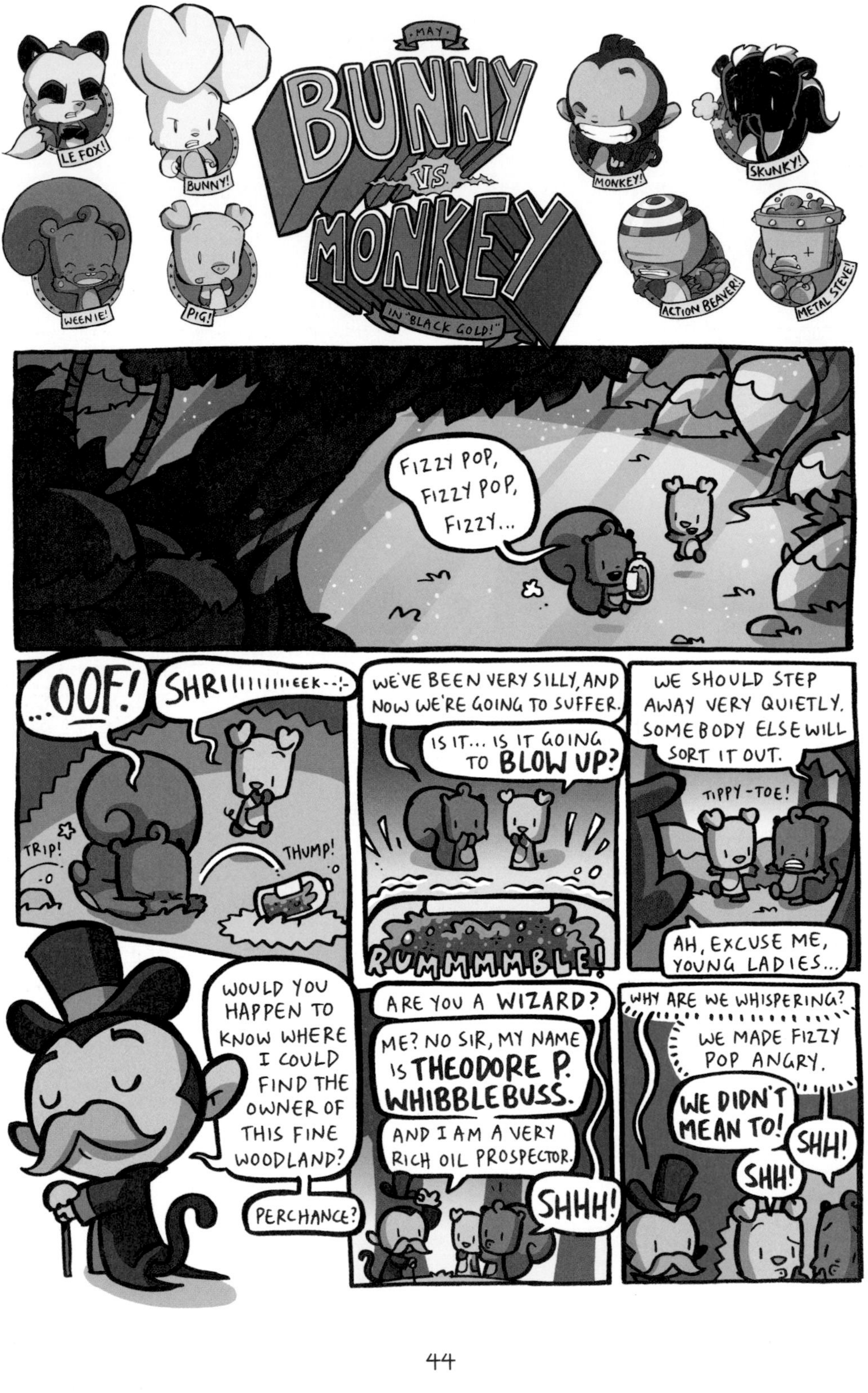
MAY
BUNNY VS MONKEY
IN "BLACK GOLD!"
LE FOX!
BUNNY!
WEENIE!
PIG!
MONKEY!
SKUNKY!
ACTION BEAVER!
METAL STEVE!
FIZZY POP, FIZZY POP, FIZZY...
...OOF!
SHRIIIIIIIIIEEK--
TRIP!
THUMP!
WE'VE BEEN VERY SILLY, AND NOW WE'RE GOING TO SUFFER.
IS IT... IS IT GOING TO BLOW UP?
RUMMMMBLE!
WE SHOULD STEP AWAY VERY QUIETLY. SOMEBODY ELSE WILL SORT IT OUT.
TIPPY-TOE!
AH, EXCUSE ME, YOUNG LADIES...
WOULD YOU HAPPEN TO KNOW WHERE I COULD FIND THE OWNER OF THIS FINE WOODLAND?
PERCHANCE?
ARE YOU A WIZARD?
ME? NO SIR, MY NAME IS THEODORE P. WHIBBLEBUSS.
AND I AM A VERY RICH OIL PROSPECTOR.
SHHH!
WHY ARE WE WHISPERING?
WE MADE FIZZY POP ANGRY.
WE DIDN'T MEAN TO!
SHH!
SHH!

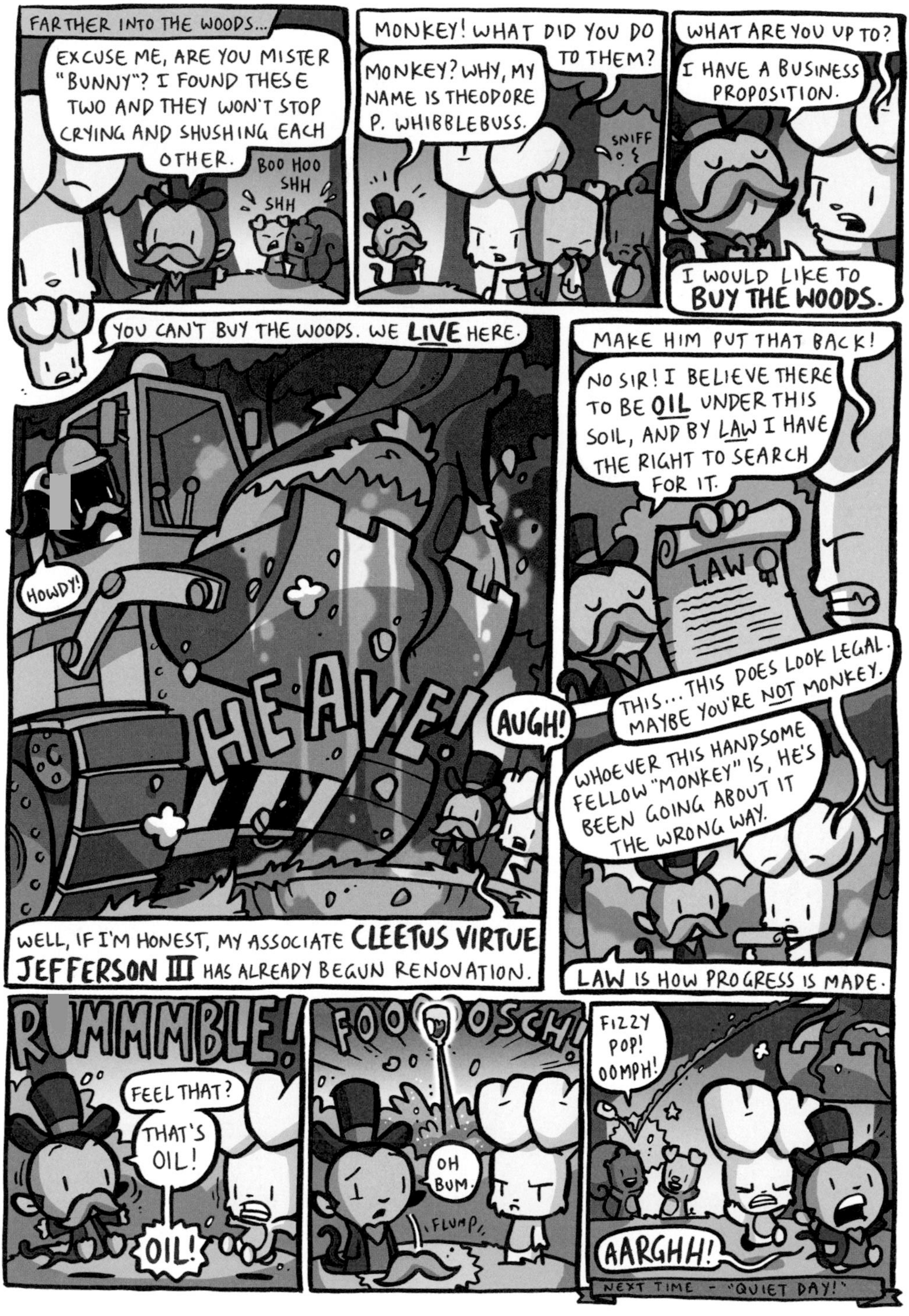

FARTHER INTO THE WOODS...
EXCUSE ME, ARE YOU MISTER "BUNNY"? I FOUND THESE TWO AND THEY WON'T STOP CRYING AND SHUSHING EACH OTHER.
BOO HOO
SHH
SHH
MONKEY! WHAT DID YOU DO TO THEM?
MONKEY? WHY, MY NAME IS THEODORE P. WHIBBLEBUSS.
SNIFF
WHAT ARE YOU UP TO?
I HAVE A BUSINESS PROPOSITION.
I WOULD LIKE TO BUY THE WOODS.
YOU CAN'T BUY THE WOODS. WE LIVE HERE.
HOWDY!
HEAVE!
AUGH!
WELL, IF I'M HONEST, MY ASSOCIATE CLEETUS VIRTUE JEFFERSON III HAS ALREADY BEGUN RENOVATION.
MAKE HIM PUT THAT BACK!
NO SIR! I BELIEVE THERE TO BE OIL UNDER THIS SOIL, AND BY LAW I HAVE THE RIGHT TO SEARCH FOR IT.
LAW
THIS... THIS DOES LOOK LEGAL. MAYBE YOU'RE NOT MONKEY.
WHOEVER THIS HANDSOME FELLOW "MONKEY" IS, HE'S BEEN GOING ABOUT IT THE WRONG WAY.
LAW IS HOW PROGRESS IS MADE.
RUMMMBLE!
FEEL THAT?
THAT'S OIL!
OIL!
FOOOOOSCH!
OH BUM.
FLUMP
FIZZY POP! OOMPH!
AARGHH!
NEXT TIME - "QUIET DAY!"

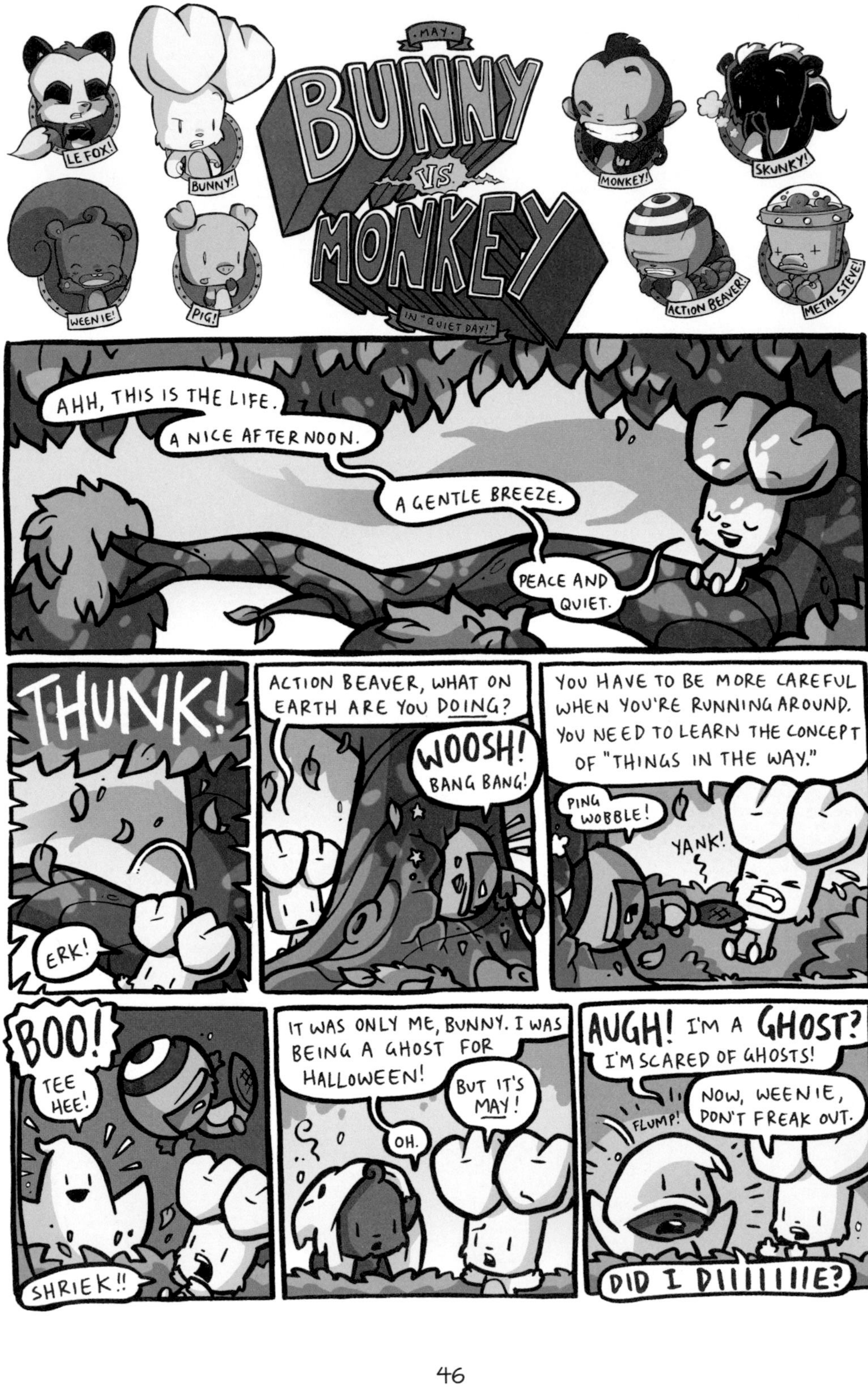
LE FOX!
BUNNY!
WEENIE!
PIG!
MAY
BUNNY VS MONKEY
IN "QUIET DAY!"
MONKEY!
SKUNKY!
ACTION BEAVER!
METAL STEVE!
AHH, THIS IS THE LIFE.
A NICE AFTERNOON.
A GENTLE BREEZE.
PEACE AND QUIET.
THUNK!
ERK!
ACTION BEAVER, WHAT ON EARTH ARE YOU DOING?
WOOSH! BANG BANG!
YOU HAVE TO BE MORE CAREFUL WHEN YOU'RE RUNNING AROUND. YOU NEED TO LEARN THE CONCEPT OF "THINGS IN THE WAY."
PING WOBBLE!
YANK!
BOO!
TEE HEE!
SHRIEK!!
IT WAS ONLY ME, BUNNY. I WAS BEING A GHOST FOR HALLOWEEN!
BUT IT'S MAY!
OH.
AUGH! I'M A GHOST? I'M SCARED OF GHOSTS!
NOW, WEENIE, DON'T FREAK OUT.
FLUMP!
DID I DIIIIIIIE?

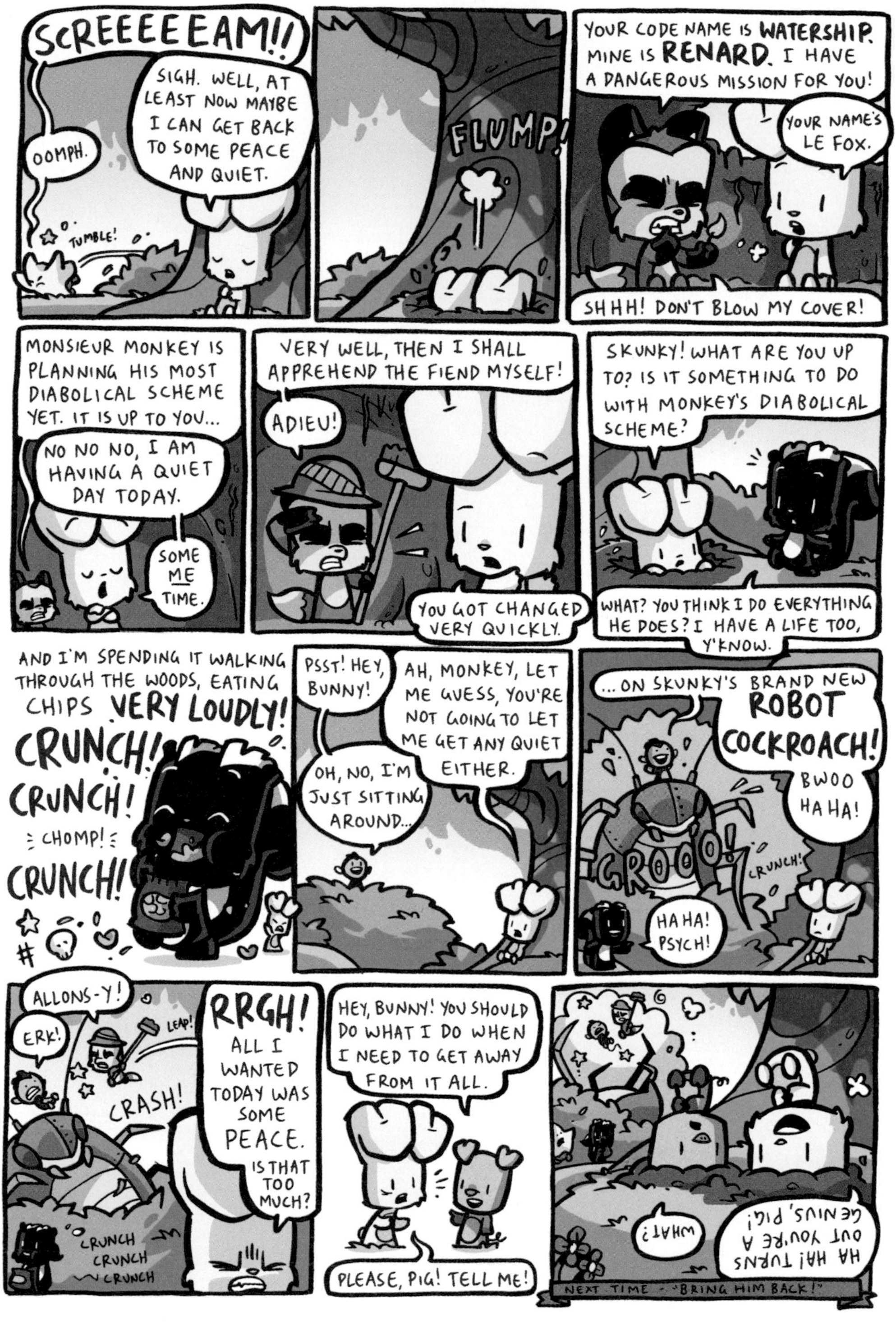
SCREEEEEAM!!
OOMPH.
SIGH. WELL, AT LEAST NOW MAYBE I CAN GET BACK TO SOME PEACE AND QUIET.
TUMBLE!
FLUMP!
YOUR CODE NAME IS WATERSHIP. MINE IS RENARD. I HAVE A DANGEROUS MISSION FOR YOU!
YOUR NAME'S LE FOX.
SHHH! DON'T BLOW MY COVER!
MONSIEUR MONKEY IS PLANNING HIS MOST DIABOLICAL SCHEME YET. IT IS UP TO YOU...
NO NO NO, I AM HAVING A QUIET DAY TODAY.
SOME ME TIME.
VERY WELL, THEN I SHALL APPREHEND THE FIEND MYSELF!
ADIEU!
YOU GOT CHANGED VERY QUICKLY.
SKUNKY! WHAT ARE YOU UP TO? IS IT SOMETHING TO DO WITH MONKEY'S DIABOLICAL SCHEME?
WHAT? YOU THINK I DO EVERYTHING HE DOES? I HAVE A LIFE TOO, Y'KNOW.
AND I'M SPENDING IT WALKING THROUGH THE WOODS, EATING CHIPS VERY LOUDLY!
CRUNCH!
CRUNCH!
CHOMP!
CRUNCH!
PSST! HEY, BUNNY!
AH, MONKEY, LET ME GUESS, YOU'RE NOT GOING TO LET ME GET ANY QUIET EITHER.
OH, NO, I'M JUST SITTING AROUND...
...ON SKUNKY'S BRAND NEW ROBOT COCKROACH!
BWOO HA HA!
GROOO!
CRUNCH!
HA HA! PSYCH!
ALLONS-Y!
ERK!
LEAP!
CRASH!
CRUNCH CRUNCH CRUNCH
RRGH! ALL I WANTED TODAY WAS SOME PEACE. IS THAT TOO MUCH?
HEY, BUNNY! YOU SHOULD DO WHAT I DO WHEN I NEED TO GET AWAY FROM IT ALL.
PLEASE, PIG! TELL ME!
HA HA! TURNS OUT YOU'RE A GENIUS, PIG!
WHAT?
NEXT TIME - "BRING HIM BACK!"

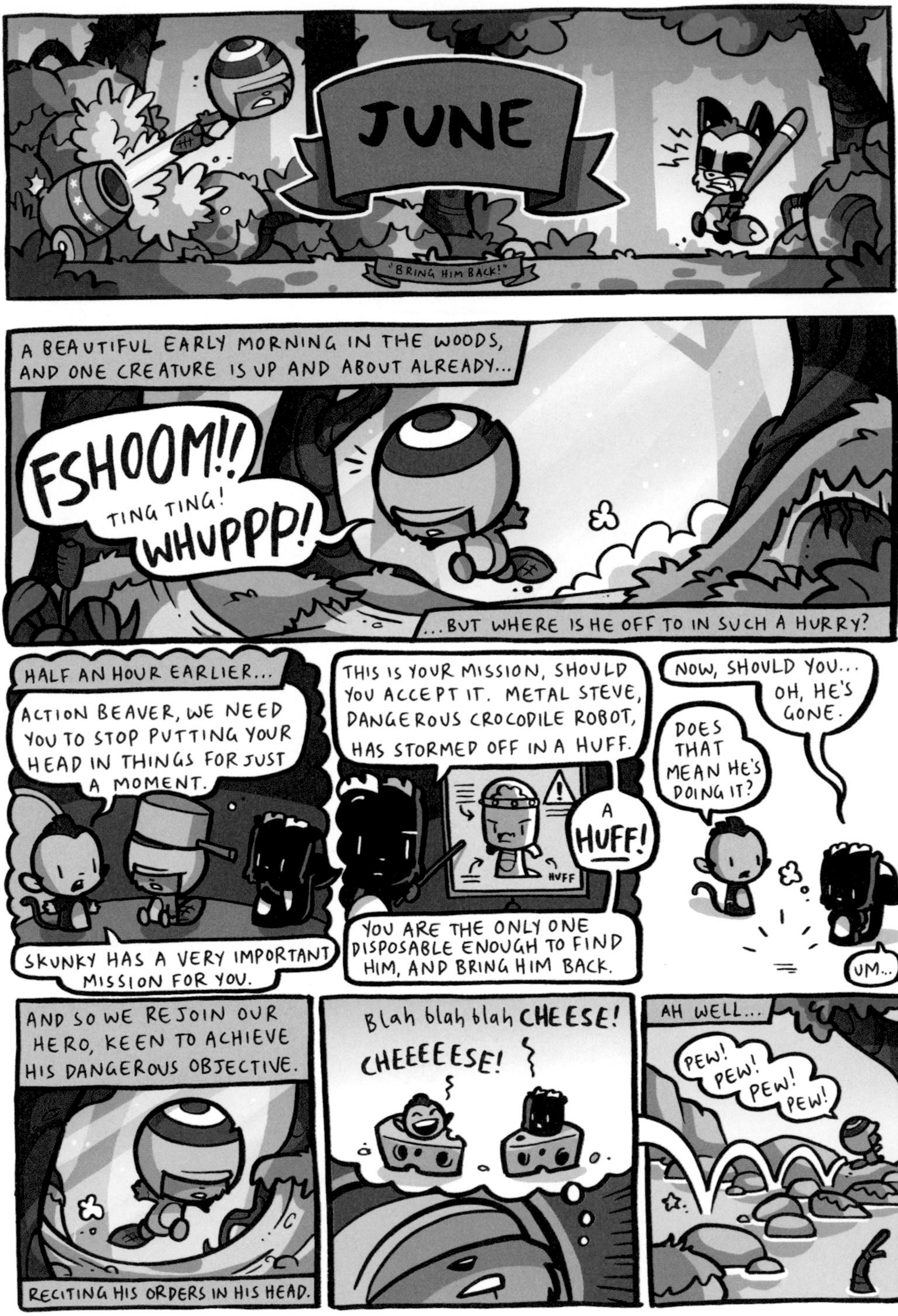
JUNE
"BRING HIM BACK!"
A BEAUTIFUL EARLY MORNING IN THE WOODS, AND ONE CREATURE IS UP AND ABOUT ALREADY...
FSHOOM!! TING TING! WHUPPP!
...BUT WHERE IS HE OFF TO IN SUCH A HURRY?
HALF AN HOUR EARLIER...
ACTION BEAVER, WE NEED YOU TO STOP PUTTING YOUR HEAD IN THINGS FOR JUST A MOMENT.
SKUNKY HAS A VERY IMPORTANT MISSION FOR YOU.
THIS IS YOUR MISSION, SHOULD YOU ACCEPT IT. METAL STEVE, DANGEROUS CROCODILE ROBOT, HAS STORMED OFF IN A HUFF.
A HUFF!
HUFF
YOU ARE THE ONLY ONE DISPOSABLE ENOUGH TO FIND HIM, AND BRING HIM BACK.
NOW, SHOULD YOU... OH, HE'S GONE.
DOES THAT MEAN HE'S DOING IT?
UM...
AND SO WE REJOIN OUR HERO, KEEN TO ACHIEVE HIS DANGEROUS OBJECTIVE.
RECITING HIS ORDERS IN HIS HEAD.
Blah blah blah CHEESE!
CHEEEEESE!
AH WELL...
PEW! PEW! PEW! PEW!

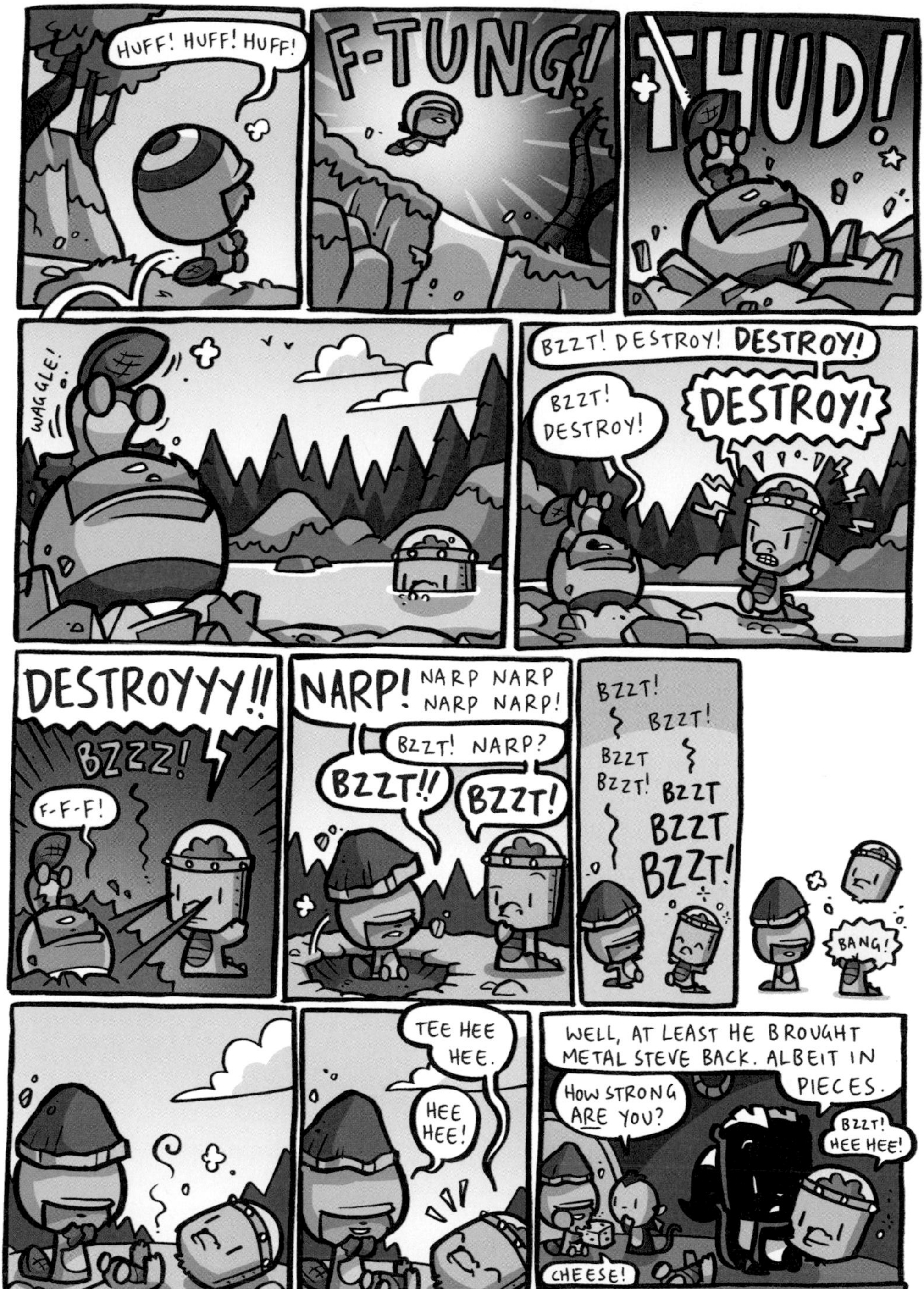
HUFF! HUFF! HUFF!
F-TUNG!
THUD!
WAGGLE!
BZZT! DESTROY! DESTROY!
BZZT! DESTROY!
DESTROY!
DESTROYYY!!
BZZZ!
F-F-F!
NARP! NARP NARP NARP NARP!
BZZT! NARP?
BZZT!!
BZZT!
BZZT!
BZZT!
BZZT BZZT!
BZZT BZZT BZZT!
BANG!
TEE HEE HEE.
HEE HEE!
WELL, AT LEAST HE BROUGHT METAL STEVE BACK. ALBEIT IN PIECES.
HOW STRONG ARE YOU?
BZZT! HEE HEE!
CHEESE!
NEXT TIME - "WHO'S AFRAID OF THE BIG BAD BEAR?"

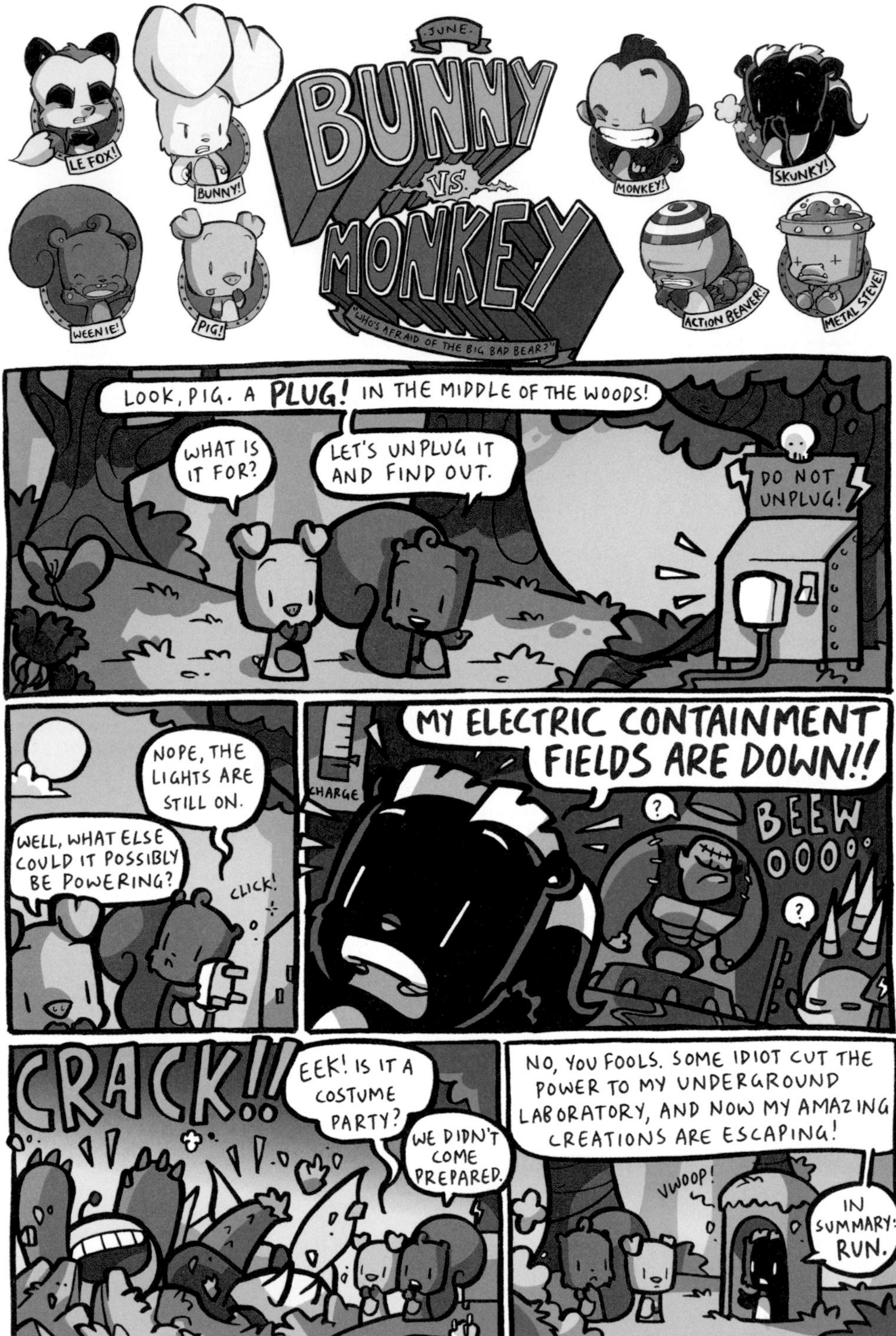
LE FOX!
BUNNY!
JUNE
BUNNY VS. MONKEY
"WHO'S AFRAID OF THE BIG BAD BEAR?"
MONKEY!
SKUNKY!
WEENIE!
PIG!
ACTION BEAVER!
METAL STEVE!
LOOK, PIG. A PLUG! IN THE MIDDLE OF THE WOODS!
WHAT IS IT FOR?
LET'S UNPLUG IT AND FIND OUT.
DO NOT UNPLUG!
NOPE, THE LIGHTS ARE STILL ON.
WELL, WHAT ELSE COULD IT POSSIBLY BE POWERING?
CLICK!
MY ELECTRIC CONTAINMENT FIELDS ARE DOWN!!
CHARGE
?
BEEW OOOO
?
CRACK!!
EEK! IS IT A COSTUME PARTY?
WE DIDN'T COME PREPARED.
NO, YOU FOOLS. SOME IDIOT CUT THE POWER TO MY UNDERGROUND LABORATORY, AND NOW MY AMAZING CREATIONS ARE ESCAPING!
VWOOP!
IN SUMMARY: RUN.

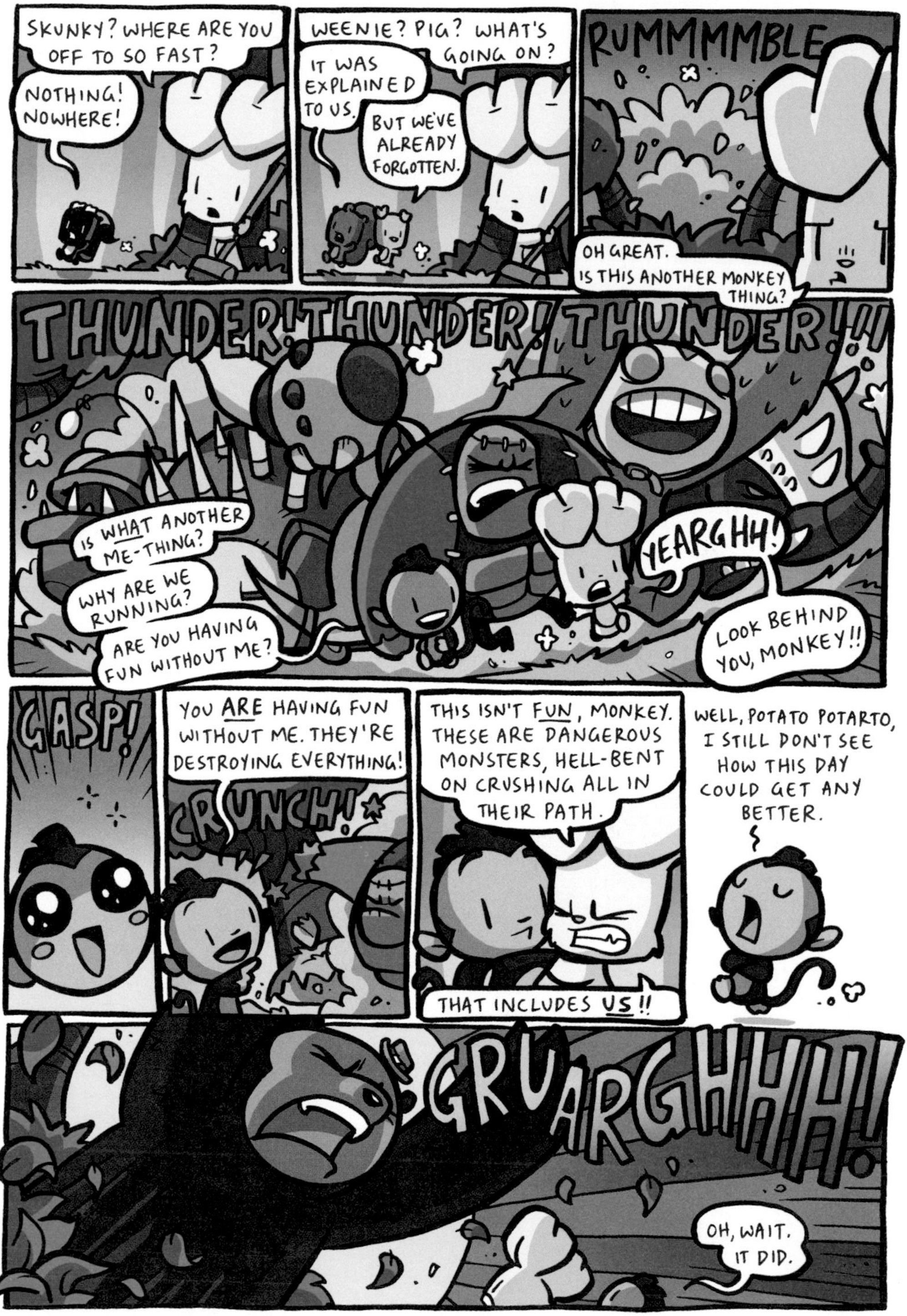

SKUNKY? WHERE ARE YOU OFF TO SO FAST?
NOTHING! NOWHERE!
WEENIE? PIG? WHAT'S GOING ON?
IT WAS EXPLAINED TO US.
BUT WE'VE ALREADY FORGOTTEN.
RUMMMMBLE
OH GREAT. IS THIS ANOTHER MONKEY THING?
THUNDER! THUNDER! THUNDER!!!
IS WHAT ANOTHER ME-THING?
WHY ARE WE RUNNING?
ARE YOU HAVING FUN WITHOUT ME?
YEARGHH!
LOOK BEHIND YOU, MONKEY!!
GASP!
YOU ARE HAVING FUN WITHOUT ME. THEY'RE DESTROYING EVERYTHING!
CRUNCH!
THIS ISN'T FUN, MONKEY. THESE ARE DANGEROUS MONSTERS, HELL-BENT ON CRUSHING ALL IN THEIR PATH.
THAT INCLUDES US!!
WELL, POTATO POTARTO, I STILL DON'T SEE HOW THIS DAY COULD GET ANY BETTER.
GRUARGHHH!
OH, WAIT. IT DID.

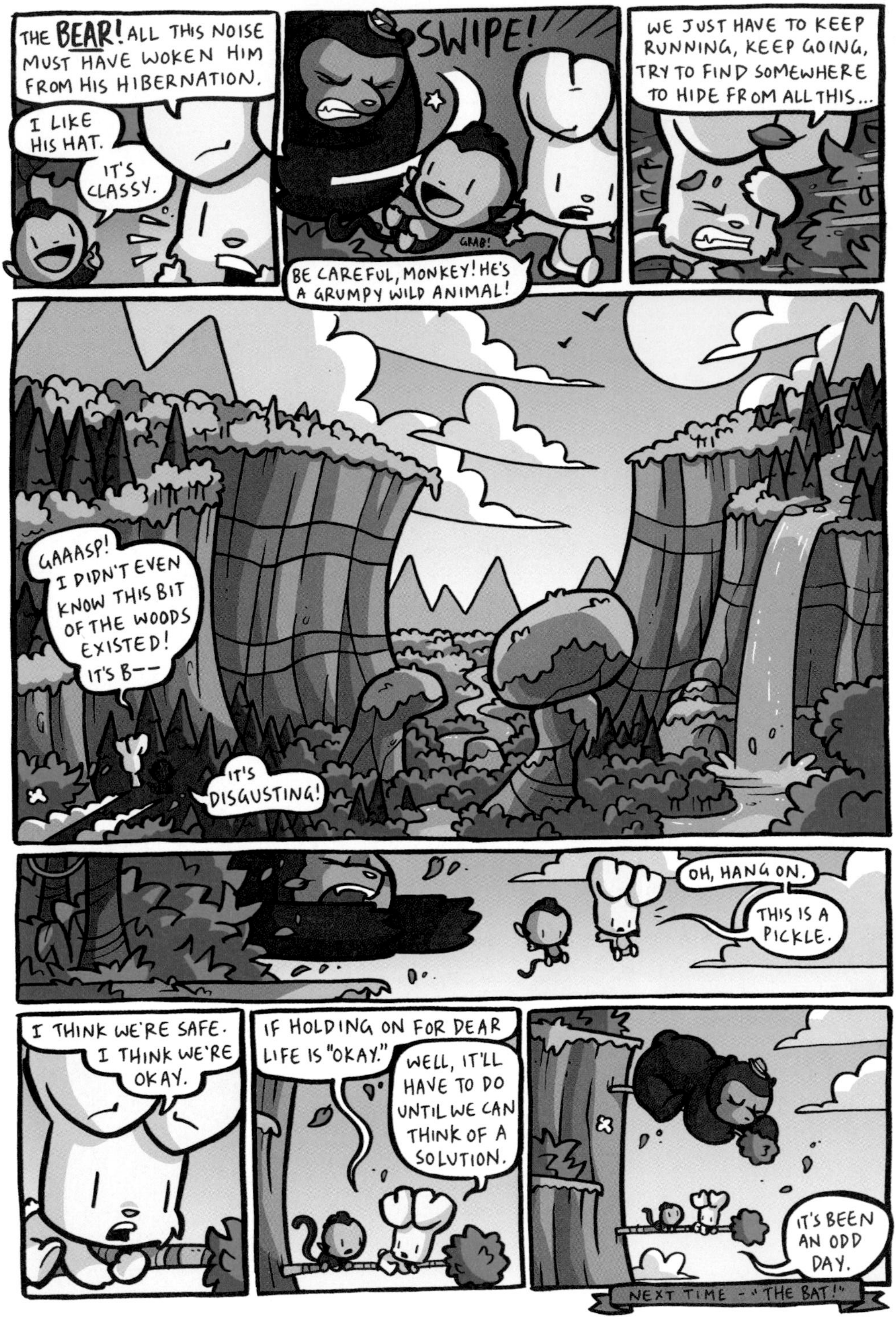
THE BEAR! ALL THIS NOISE MUST HAVE WOKEN HIM FROM HIS HIBERNATION.
I LIKE HIS HAT.
IT'S CLASSY.
SWIPE!
GRAB!
BE CAREFUL, MONKEY! HE'S A GRUMPY WILD ANIMAL!
WE JUST HAVE TO KEEP RUNNING, KEEP GOING, TRY TO FIND SOMEWHERE TO HIDE FROM ALL THIS...
GAAASP! I DIDN'T EVEN KNOW THIS BIT OF THE WOODS EXISTED! IT'S B--
IT'S DISGUSTING!
OH, HANG ON.
THIS IS A PICKLE.
I THINK WE'RE SAFE. I THINK WE'RE OKAY.
IF HOLDING ON FOR DEAR LIFE IS "OKAY."
WELL, IT'LL HAVE TO DO UNTIL WE CAN THINK OF A SOLUTION.
IT'S BEEN AN ODD DAY.
NEXT TIME - "THE BAT!"

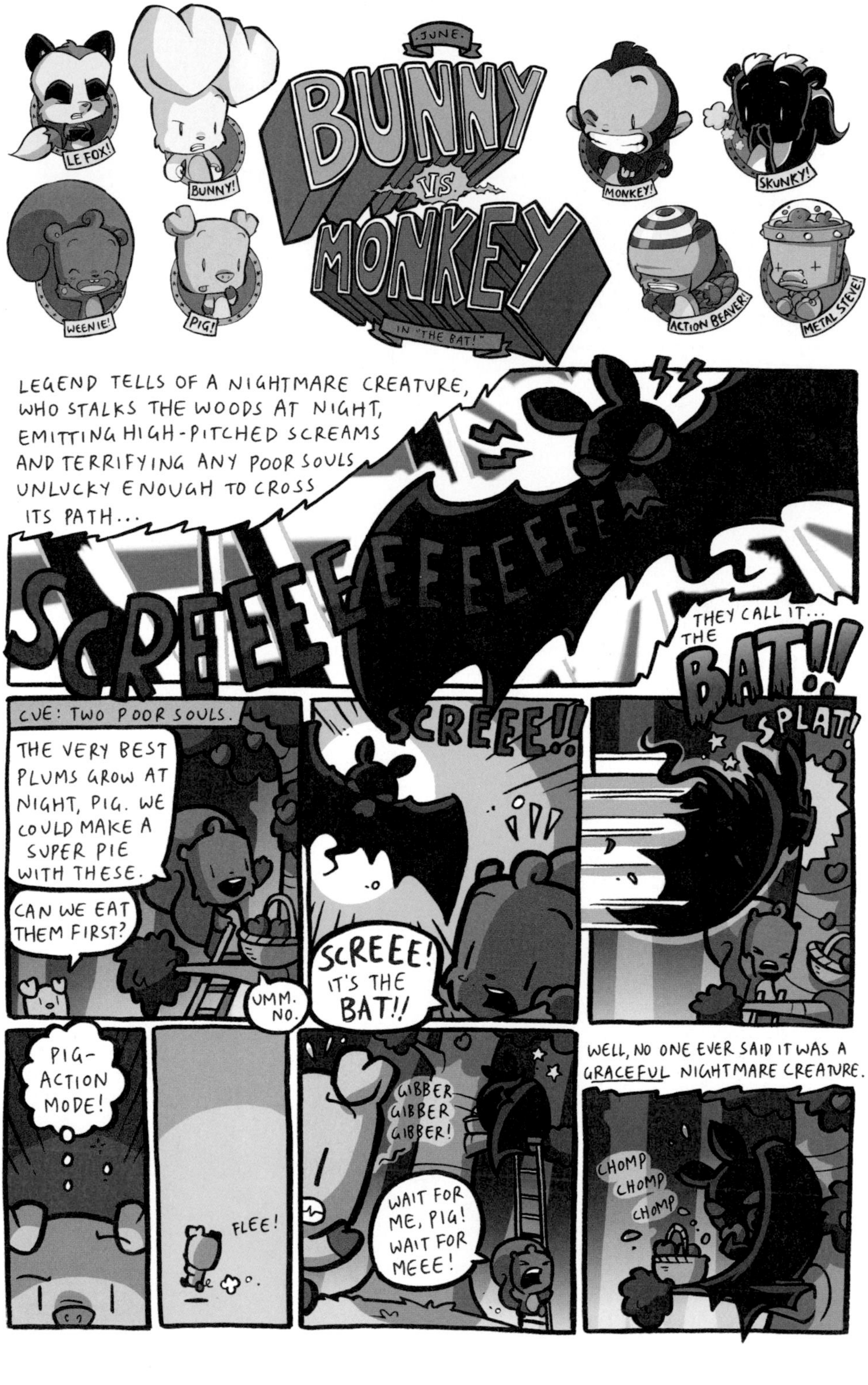

·JUNE·
BUNNY VS. MONKEY
IN "THE BAT!"
LE FOX!
BUNNY!
MONKEY!
SKUNKY!
WEENIE!
PIG!
ACTION BEAVER!
METAL STEVE!
LEGEND TELLS OF A NIGHTMARE CREATURE, WHO STALKS THE WOODS AT NIGHT, EMITTING HIGH-PITCHED SCREAMS AND TERRIFYING ANY POOR SOULS UNLUCKY ENOUGH TO CROSS ITS PATH...
SCREEEEEEEEEEE
THEY CALL IT... THE
BAT!!
CUE: TWO POOR SOULS.
THE VERY BEST PLUMS GROW AT NIGHT, PIG. WE COULD MAKE A SUPER PIE WITH THESE.
CAN WE EAT THEM FIRST?
UMM. NO.
SCREEE!!
SCREEE! IT'S THE BAT!!
SPLAT!
PIG-ACTION MODE!
FLEE!
GIBBER GIBBER GIBBER!
WAIT FOR ME, PIG! WAIT FOR MEEE!
WELL, NO ONE EVER SAID IT WAS A GRACEFUL NIGHTMARE CREATURE.
CHOMP
CHOMP
CHOMP

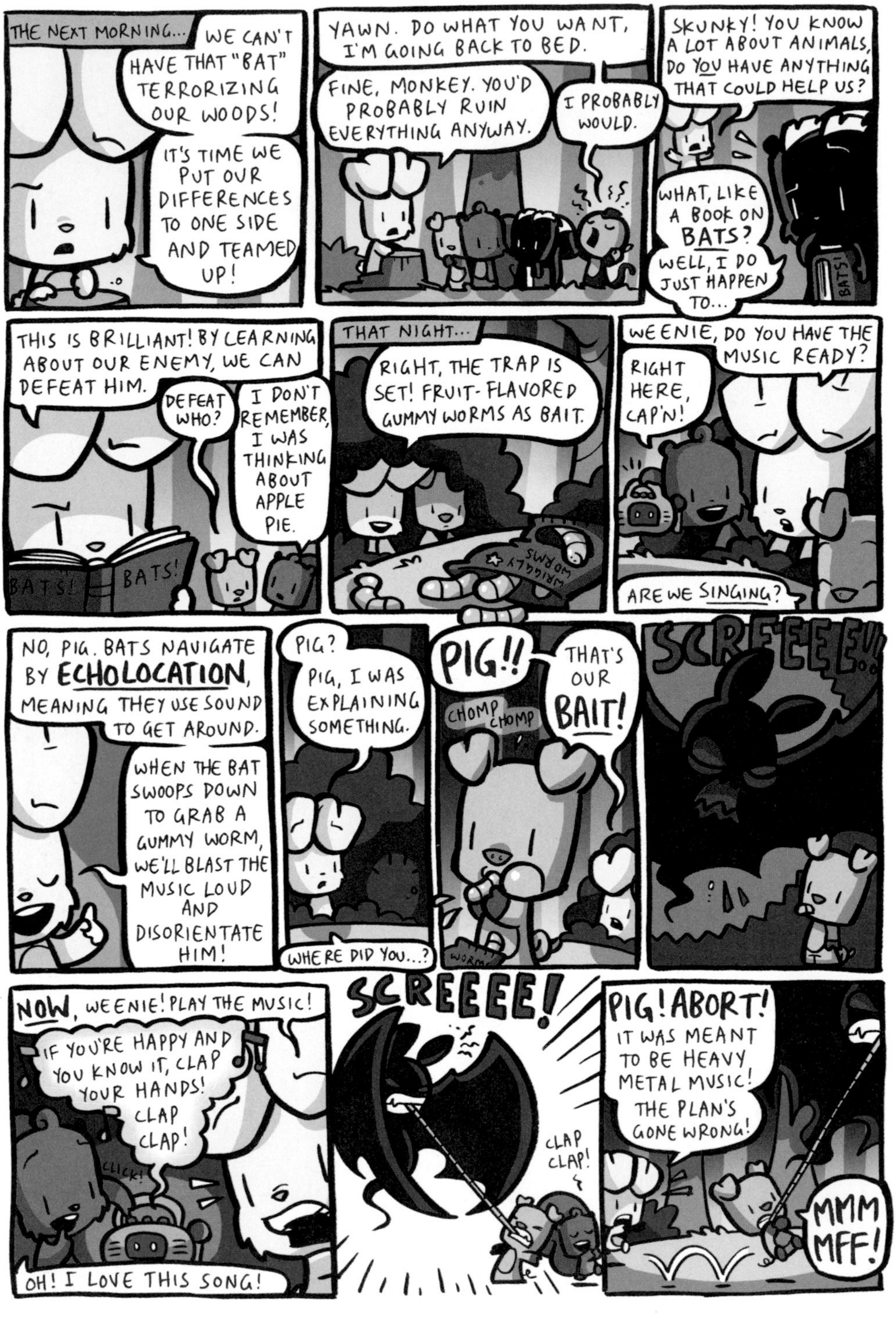
THE NEXT MORNING...
WE CAN'T HAVE THAT "BAT" TERRORIZING OUR WOODS!
IT'S TIME WE PUT OUR DIFFERENCES TO ONE SIDE AND TEAMED UP!
YAWN. DO WHAT YOU WANT, I'M GOING BACK TO BED.
FINE, MONKEY. YOU'D PROBABLY RUIN EVERYTHING ANYWAY.
I PROBABLY WOULD.
SKUNKY! YOU KNOW A LOT ABOUT ANIMALS, DO YOU HAVE ANYTHING THAT COULD HELP US?
WHAT, LIKE A BOOK ON BATS?
WELL, I DO JUST HAPPEN TO...
BATS!
THIS IS BRILLIANT! BY LEARNING ABOUT OUR ENEMY, WE CAN DEFEAT HIM.
DEFEAT WHO?
I DON'T REMEMBER, I WAS THINKING ABOUT APPLE PIE.
BATS!
BATS!
THAT NIGHT...
RIGHT, THE TRAP IS SET! FRUIT-FLAVORED GUMMY WORMS AS BAIT.
WRIGGLY WORMS
WEENIE, DO YOU HAVE THE MUSIC READY?
RIGHT HERE, CAP'N!
ARE WE SINGING?
NO, PIG. BATS NAVIGATE BY ECHOLOCATION, MEANING THEY USE SOUND TO GET AROUND.
WHEN THE BAT SWOOPS DOWN TO GRAB A GUMMY WORM, WE'LL BLAST THE MUSIC LOUD AND DISORIENTATE HIM!
PIG?
PIG, I WAS EXPLAINING SOMETHING.
WHERE DID YOU...?
PIG!!
CHOMP CHOMP
THAT'S OUR BAIT!
SCREEEE!!
NOW, WEENIE! PLAY THE MUSIC!
IF YOU'RE HAPPY AND YOU KNOW IT, CLAP YOUR HANDS! CLAP CLAP!
CLICK!
OH! I LOVE THIS SONG!
SCREEEE!
CLAP CLAP!
PIG! ABORT!
IT WAS MEANT TO BE HEAVY METAL MUSIC! THE PLAN'S GONE WRONG!
MMM MFF!

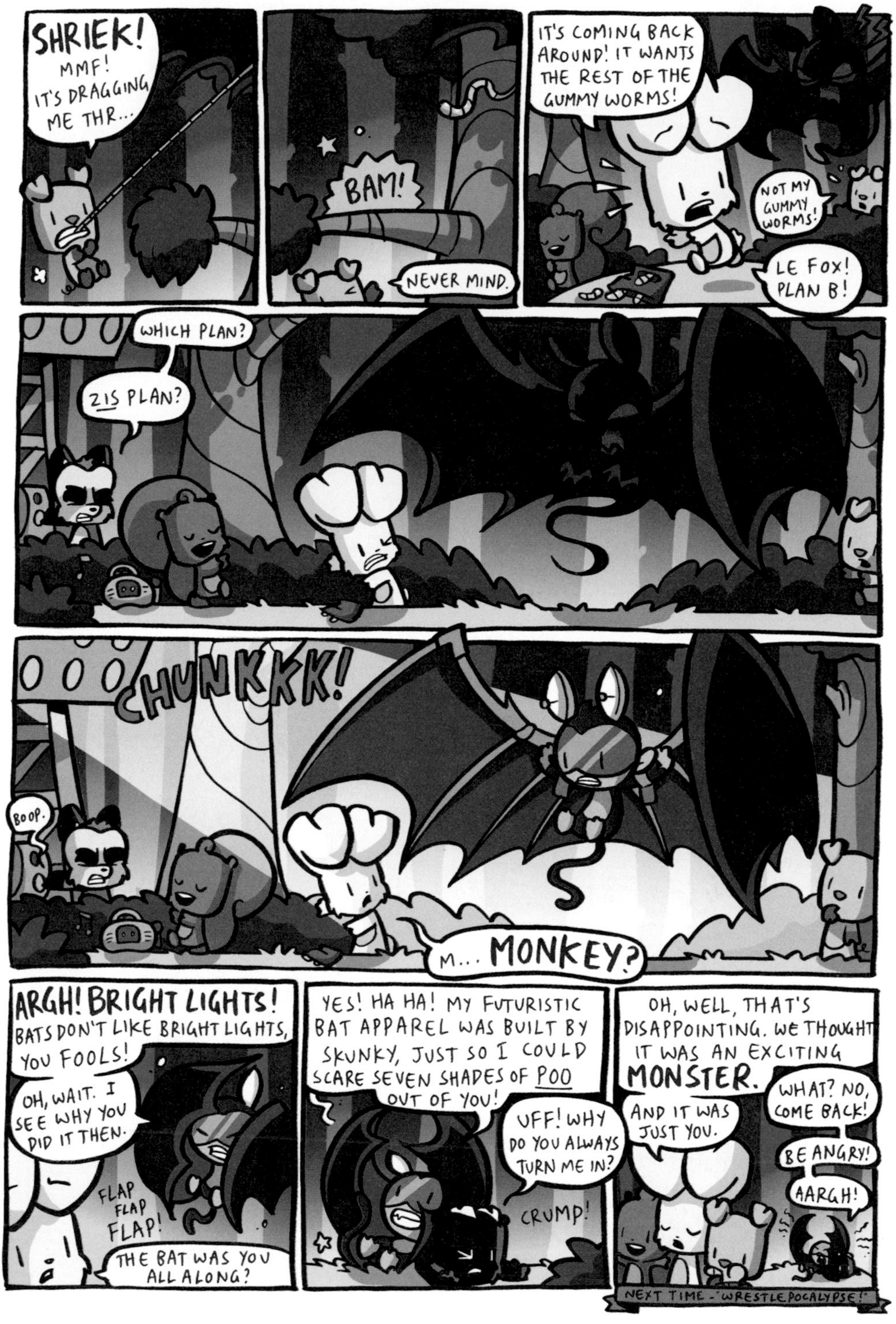
SHRIEK! MMF! IT'S DRAGGING ME THR...
BAM!
NEVER MIND.
IT'S COMING BACK AROUND! IT WANTS THE REST OF THE GUMMY WORMS!
NOT MY GUMMY WORMS!
LE FOX! PLAN B!
WHICH PLAN?
ZIS PLAN?
CHUNKKK!
BOOP.
M... MONKEY?
ARGH! BRIGHT LIGHTS! BATS DON'T LIKE BRIGHT LIGHTS, YOU FOOLS!
OH, WAIT. I SEE WHY YOU DID IT THEN.
FLAP FLAP FLAP!
THE BAT WAS YOU ALL ALONG?
YES! HA HA! MY FUTURISTIC BAT APPAREL WAS BUILT BY SKUNKY, JUST SO I COULD SCARE SEVEN SHADES OF POO OUT OF YOU!
UFF! WHY DO YOU ALWAYS TURN ME IN?
CRUMP!
OH, WELL, THAT'S DISAPPOINTING. WE THOUGHT IT WAS AN EXCITING MONSTER.
AND IT WAS JUST YOU.
WHAT? NO, COME BACK!
BE ANGRY!
AARGH!
NEXT TIME - "WRESTLEPOCALYPSE!"

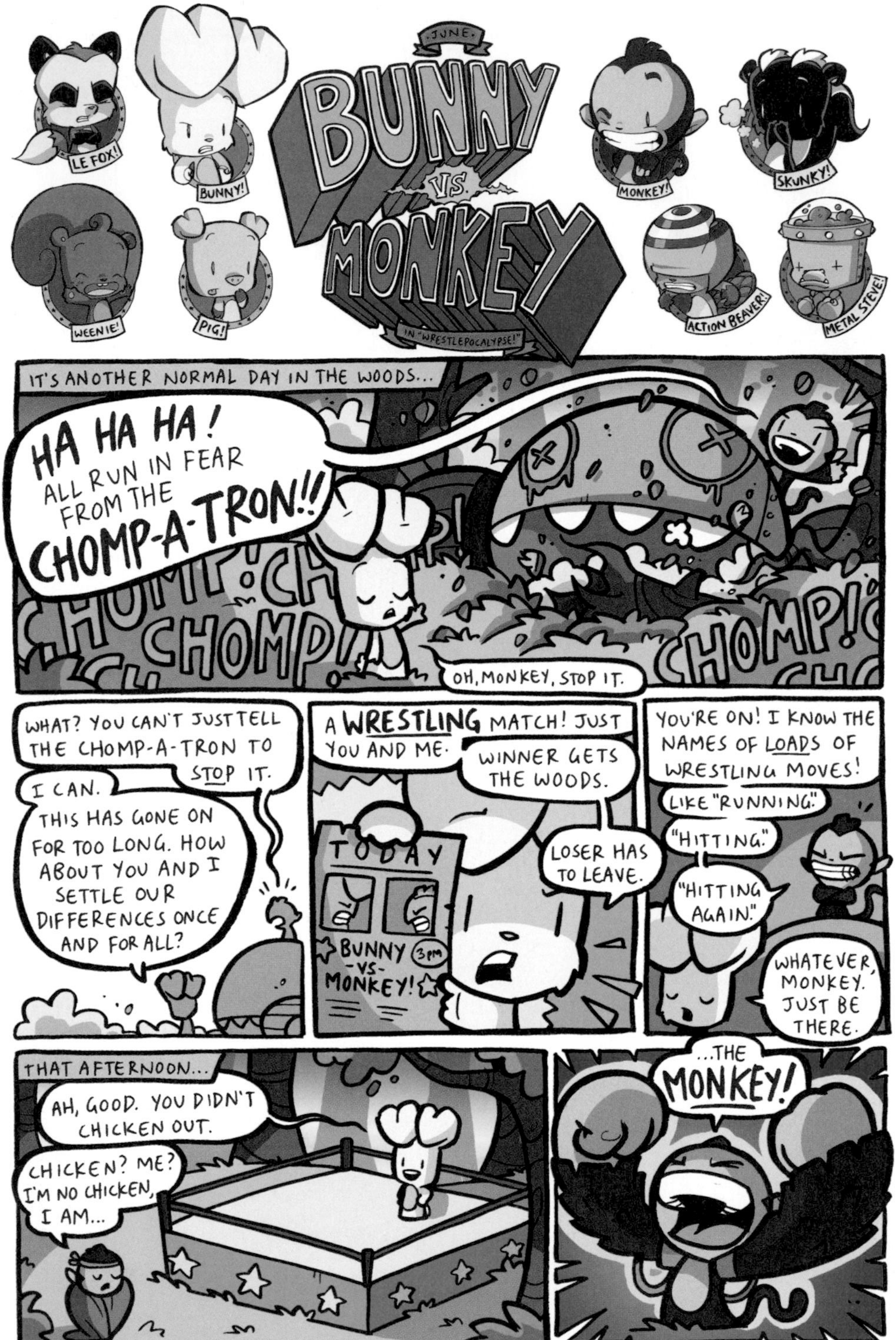
JUNE
BUNNY VS. MONKEY
IN "WRESTLEPOCALYPSE!"
LE FOX!
BUNNY!
MONKEY!
SKUNKY!
WEENIE!
PIG!
ACTION BEAVER!
METAL STEVE!
IT'S ANOTHER NORMAL DAY IN THE WOODS...
HA HA HA! ALL RUN IN FEAR FROM THE CHOMP-A-TRON!!
CHOMP! CHOMP! CHOMP! CHOMP!
OH, MONKEY, STOP IT.
WHAT? YOU CAN'T JUST TELL THE CHOMP-A-TRON TO STOP IT.
I CAN.
THIS HAS GONE ON FOR TOO LONG. HOW ABOUT YOU AND I SETTLE OUR DIFFERENCES ONCE AND FOR ALL?
A WRESTLING MATCH! JUST YOU AND ME.
WINNER GETS THE WOODS.
LOSER HAS TO LEAVE.
TODAY
BUNNY -VS- MONKEY! 3PM
YOU'RE ON! I KNOW THE NAMES OF LOADS OF WRESTLING MOVES!
LIKE "RUNNING."
"HITTING."
"HITTING AGAIN."
WHATEVER, MONKEY. JUST BE THERE.
THAT AFTERNOON...
AH, GOOD. YOU DIDN'T CHICKEN OUT.
CHICKEN? ME? I'M NO CHICKEN, I AM...
...THE MONKEY!

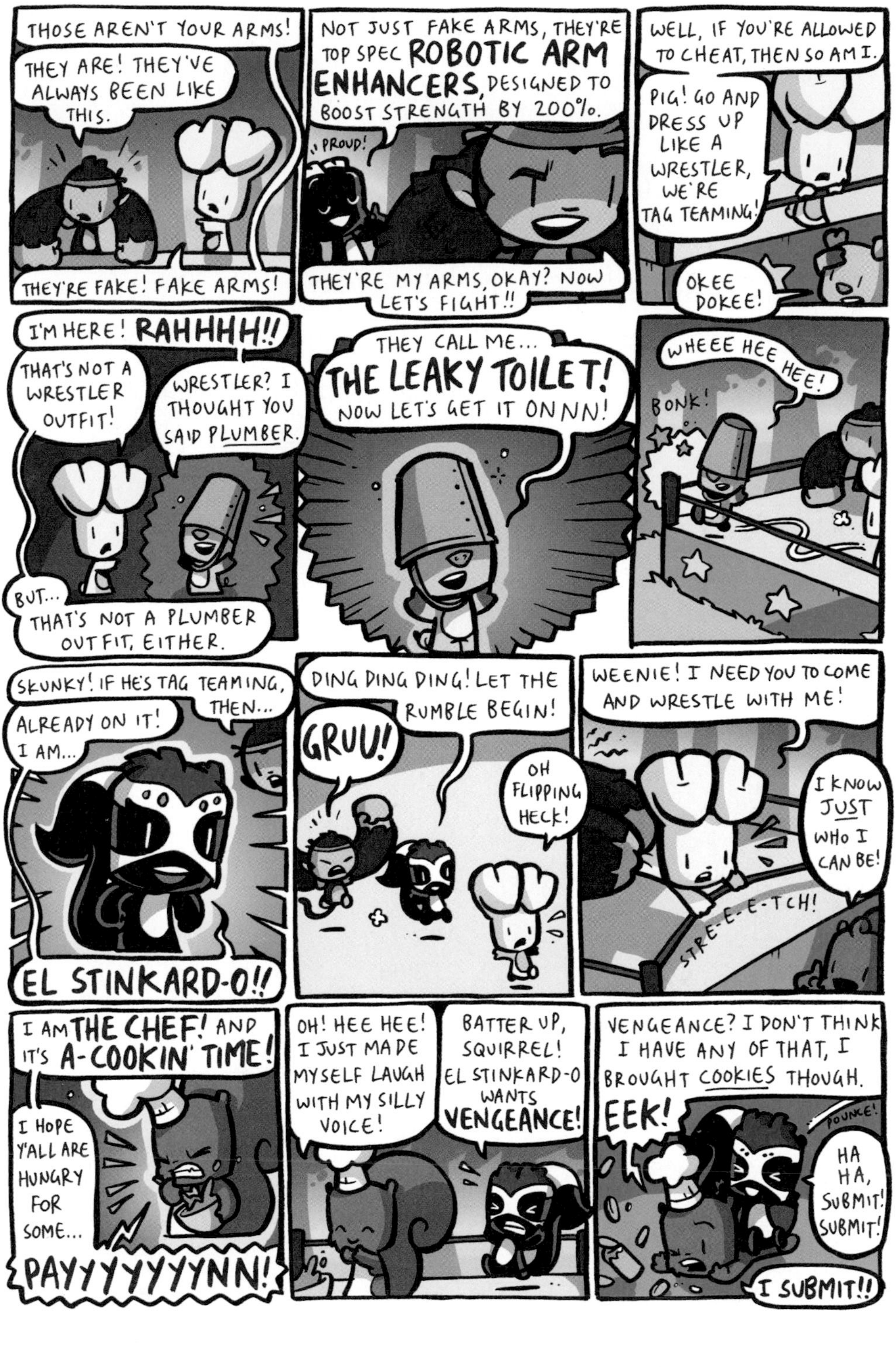
THOSE AREN'T YOUR ARMS!
THEY ARE! THEY'VE ALWAYS BEEN LIKE THIS.
THEY'RE FAKE! FAKE ARMS!
NOT JUST FAKE ARMS, THEY'RE TOP SPEC ROBOTIC ARM ENHANCERS, DESIGNED TO BOOST STRENGTH BY 200%.
PROUD!
THEY'RE MY ARMS, OKAY? NOW LET'S FIGHT!!
WELL, IF YOU'RE ALLOWED TO CHEAT, THEN SO AM I.
PIG! GO AND DRESS UP LIKE A WRESTLER, WE'RE TAG TEAMING!
OKEE DOKEE!
I'M HERE! RAHHHH!!
THAT'S NOT A WRESTLER OUTFIT!
WRESTLER? I THOUGHT YOU SAID PLUMBER.
BUT... THAT'S NOT A PLUMBER OUTFIT, EITHER.
THEY CALL ME... THE LEAKY TOILET! NOW LET'S GET IT ONNN!
WHEEE HEE HEE!
BONK!
SKUNKY! IF HE'S TAG TEAMING, THEN...
ALREADY ON IT! I AM...
EL STINKARD-O!!
DING DING DING! LET THE RUMBLE BEGIN!
GRUU!
OH FLIPPING HECK!
WEENIE! I NEED YOU TO COME AND WRESTLE WITH ME!
I KNOW JUST WHO I CAN BE!
STRE-E-E-E-TCH!
I AM THE CHEF! AND IT'S A-COOKIN' TIME!
I HOPE Y'ALL ARE HUNGRY FOR SOME...
PAYYYYYYYNN!
OH! HEE HEE! I JUST MADE MYSELF LAUGH WITH MY SILLY VOICE!
BATTER UP, SQUIRREL! EL STINKARD-O WANTS VENGEANCE!
VENGEANCE? I DON'T THINK I HAVE ANY OF THAT, I BROUGHT COOKIES THOUGH.
EEK!
POUNCE!
HA HA, SUBMIT! SUBMIT!
I SUBMIT!!

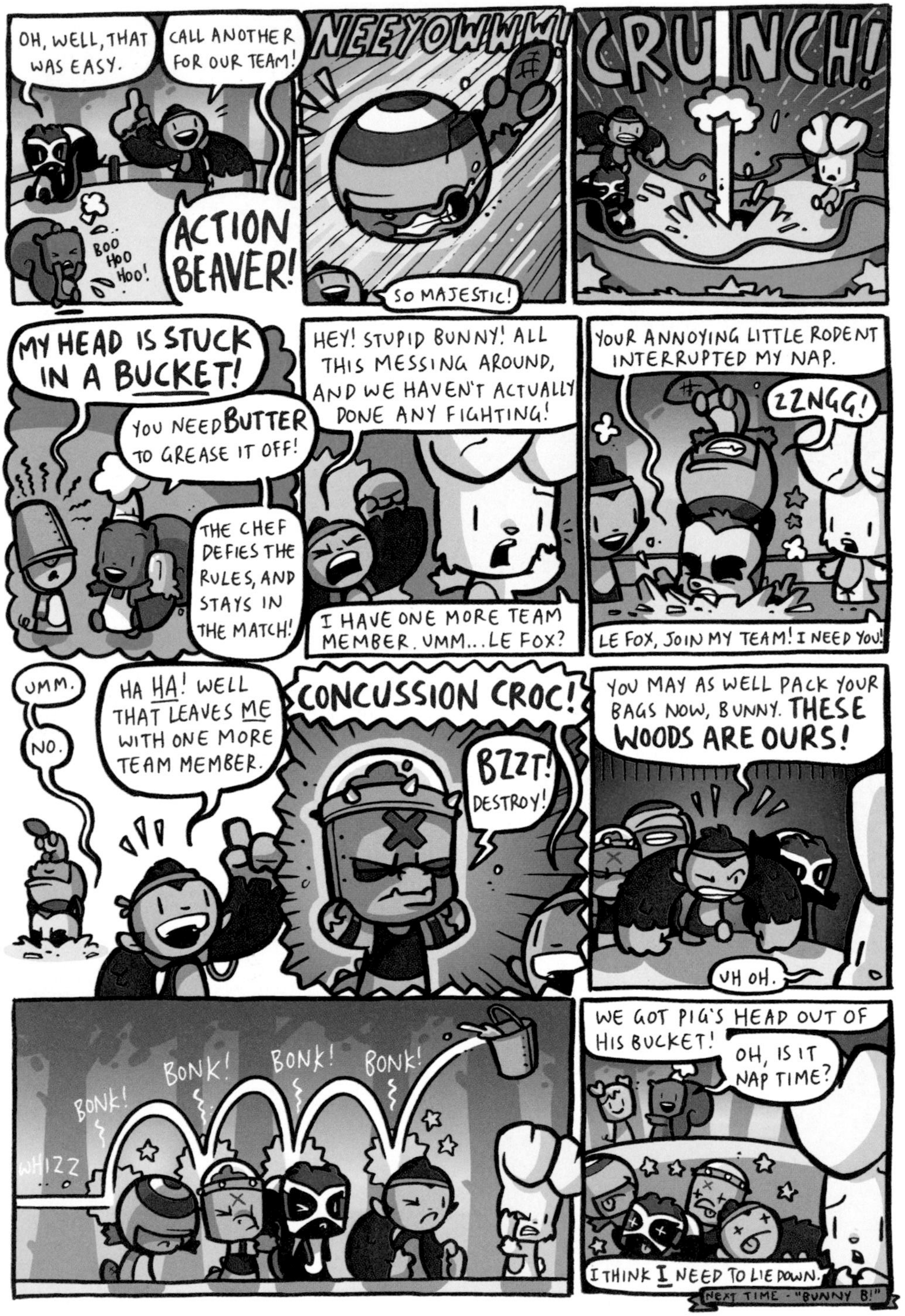
OH, WELL, THAT WAS EASY.
CALL ANOTHER FOR OUR TEAM!
BOO HOO HOO!
ACTION BEAVER!
NEEYOWWW!
SO MAJESTIC!
CRUNCH!
MY HEAD IS STUCK IN A BUCKET!
YOU NEED BUTTER TO GREASE IT OFF!
THE CHEF DEFIES THE RULES, AND STAYS IN THE MATCH!
HEY! STUPID BUNNY! ALL THIS MESSING AROUND, AND WE HAVEN'T ACTUALLY DONE ANY FIGHTING!
I HAVE ONE MORE TEAM MEMBER. UMM... LE FOX?
YOUR ANNOYING LITTLE RODENT INTERRUPTED MY NAP.
ZZNGG!
LE FOX, JOIN MY TEAM! I NEED YOU!
UMM.
NO.
HA HA! WELL THAT LEAVES ME WITH ONE MORE TEAM MEMBER.
CONCUSSION CROC!
BZZT! DESTROY!
YOU MAY AS WELL PACK YOUR BAGS NOW, BUNNY. THESE WOODS ARE OURS!
UH OH.
BONK!
BONK!
BONK!
BONK!
WHIZZ
WE GOT PIG'S HEAD OUT OF HIS BUCKET!
OH, IS IT NAP TIME?
I THINK I NEED TO LIE DOWN.
NEXT TIME - "BUNNY B!"

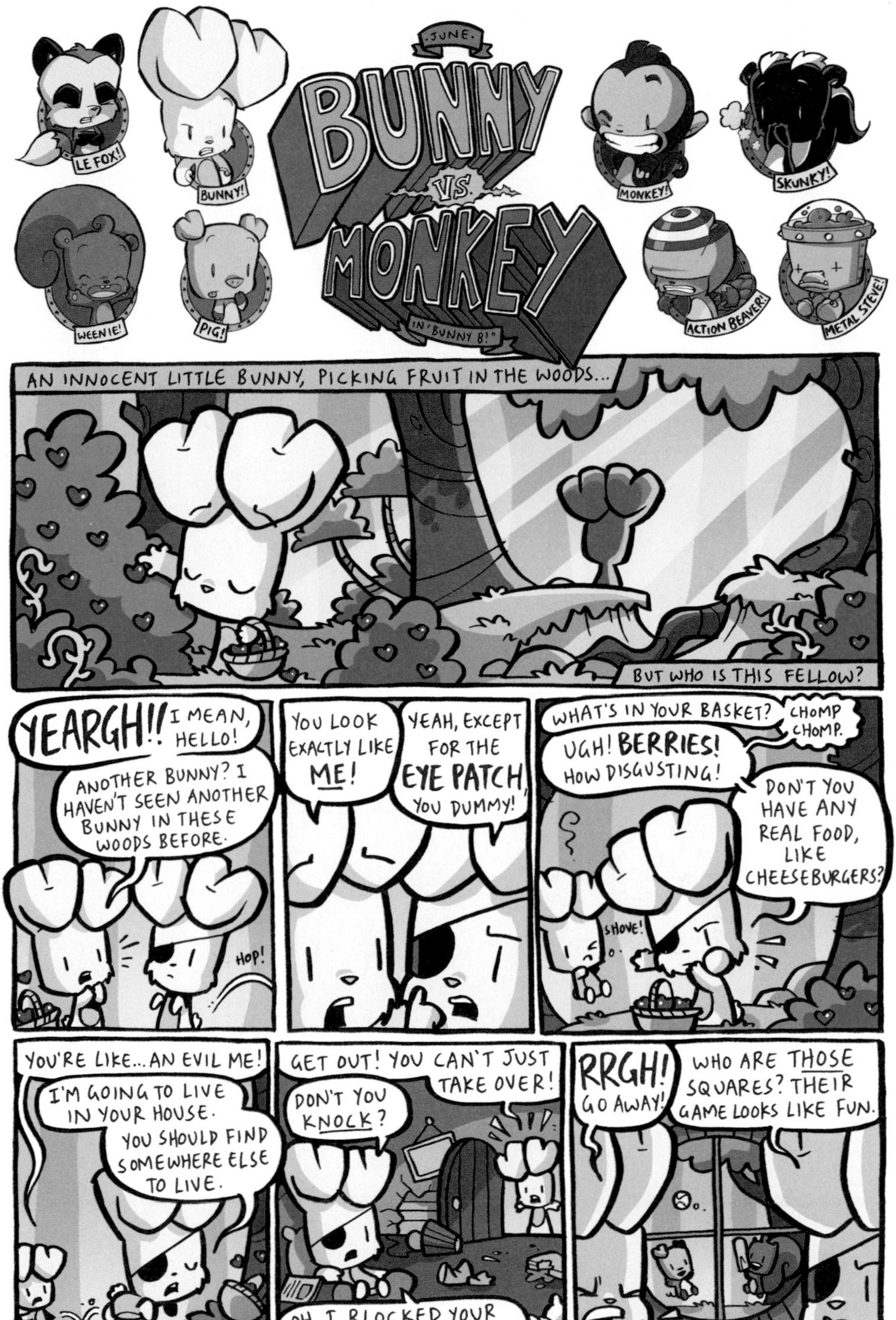
LE FOX!
BUNNY!
WEENIE!
PIG!
·JUNE·
BUNNY VS. MONKEY
IN "BUNNY 8!"
MONKEY!
SKUNKY!
ACTION BEAVER!
METAL STEVE!
AN INNOCENT LITTLE BUNNY, PICKING FRUIT IN THE WOODS...
BUT WHO IS THIS FELLOW?
YEARGH!! I MEAN, HELLO!
ANOTHER BUNNY? I HAVEN'T SEEN ANOTHER BUNNY IN THESE WOODS BEFORE.
HOP!
YOU LOOK EXACTLY LIKE ME!
YEAH, EXCEPT FOR THE EYE PATCH, YOU DUMMY!
WHAT'S IN YOUR BASKET?
CHOMP CHOMP.
UGH! BERRIES! HOW DISGUSTING!
DON'T YOU HAVE ANY REAL FOOD, LIKE CHEESEBURGERS?
SHOVE!
YOU'RE LIKE... AN EVIL ME!
I'M GOING TO LIVE IN YOUR HOUSE.
YOU SHOULD FIND SOMEWHERE ELSE TO LIVE.
GET OUT! YOU CAN'T JUST TAKE OVER!
DON'T YOU KNOCK?
OH, I BLOCKED YOUR TOILET BY THE WAY.
RRGH! GO AWAY!
WHO ARE THOSE SQUARES? THEIR GAME LOOKS LIKE FUN.

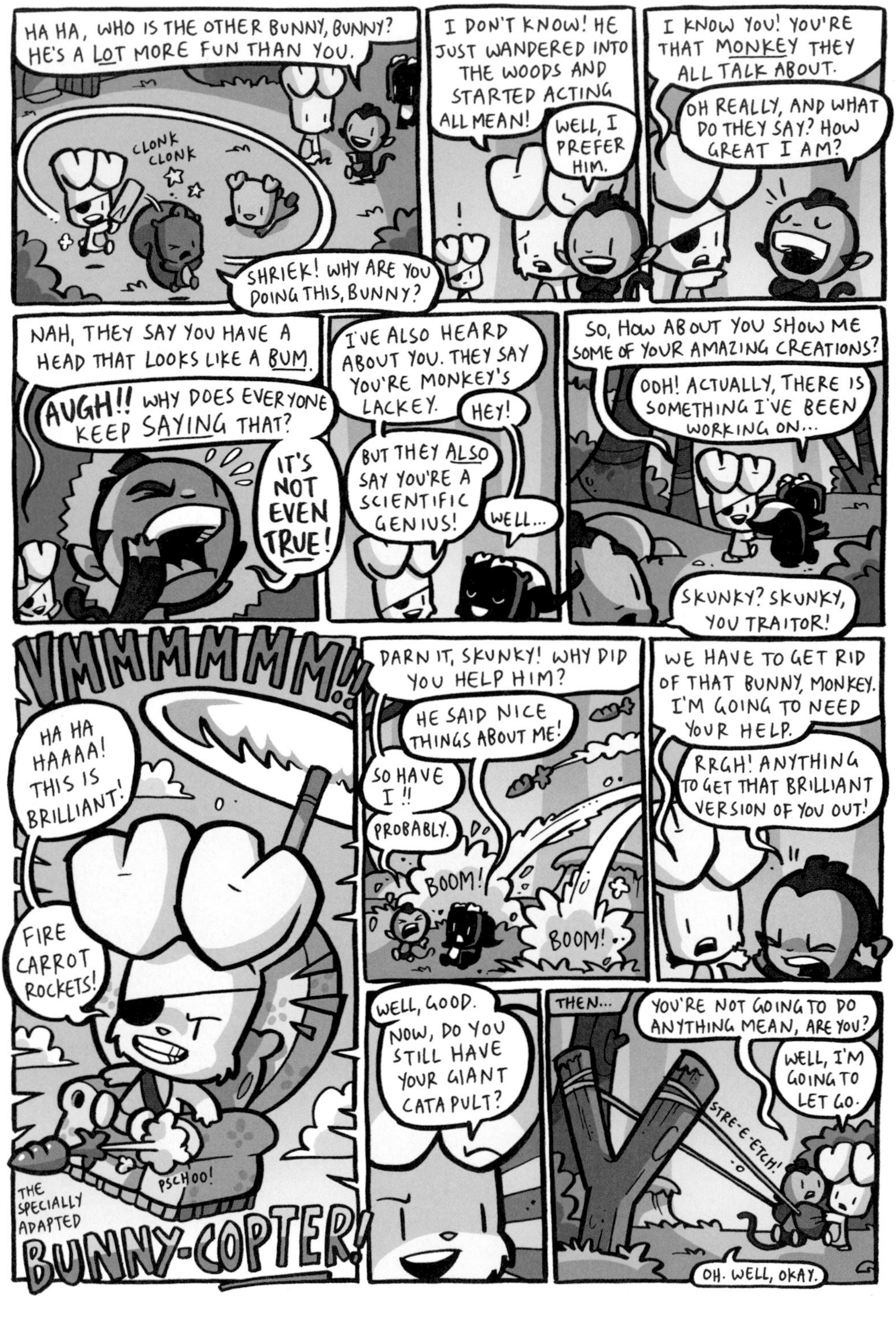
HA HA, WHO IS THE OTHER BUNNY, BUNNY? HE'S A LOT MORE FUN THAN YOU.
CLONK CLONK
SHRIEK! WHY ARE YOU DOING THIS, BUNNY?
I DON'T KNOW! HE JUST WANDERED INTO THE WOODS AND STARTED ACTING ALL MEAN!
WELL, I PREFER HIM.
I KNOW YOU! YOU'RE THAT MONKEY THEY ALL TALK ABOUT.
OH REALLY, AND WHAT DO THEY SAY? HOW GREAT I AM?
NAH, THEY SAY YOU HAVE A HEAD THAT LOOKS LIKE A BUM.
AUGH!! WHY DOES EVERYONE KEEP SAYING THAT?
IT'S NOT EVEN TRUE!
I'VE ALSO HEARD ABOUT YOU. THEY SAY YOU'RE MONKEY'S LACKEY.
HEY!
BUT THEY ALSO SAY YOU'RE A SCIENTIFIC GENIUS!
WELL...
SO, HOW ABOUT YOU SHOW ME SOME OF YOUR AMAZING CREATIONS?
OOH! ACTUALLY, THERE IS SOMETHING I'VE BEEN WORKING ON...
SKUNKY? SKUNKY, YOU TRAITOR!
VMMMMMMM!!
HA HA HAAAA! THIS IS BRILLIANT!
FIRE CARROT ROCKETS!
PSCHOO!
THE SPECIALLY ADAPTED BUNNY-COPTER!
DARN IT, SKUNKY! WHY DID YOU HELP HIM?
HE SAID NICE THINGS ABOUT ME!
SO HAVE I!!
PROBABLY.
BOOM!
BOOM!
WE HAVE TO GET RID OF THAT BUNNY, MONKEY. I'M GOING TO NEED YOUR HELP.
RRGH! ANYTHING TO GET THAT BRILLIANT VERSION OF YOU OUT!
WELL, GOOD. NOW, DO YOU STILL HAVE YOUR GIANT CATAPULT?
THEN...
YOU'RE NOT GOING TO DO ANYTHING MEAN, ARE YOU?
WELL, I'M GOING TO LET GO.
STRE-E-ETCH!
OH. WELL, OKAY.

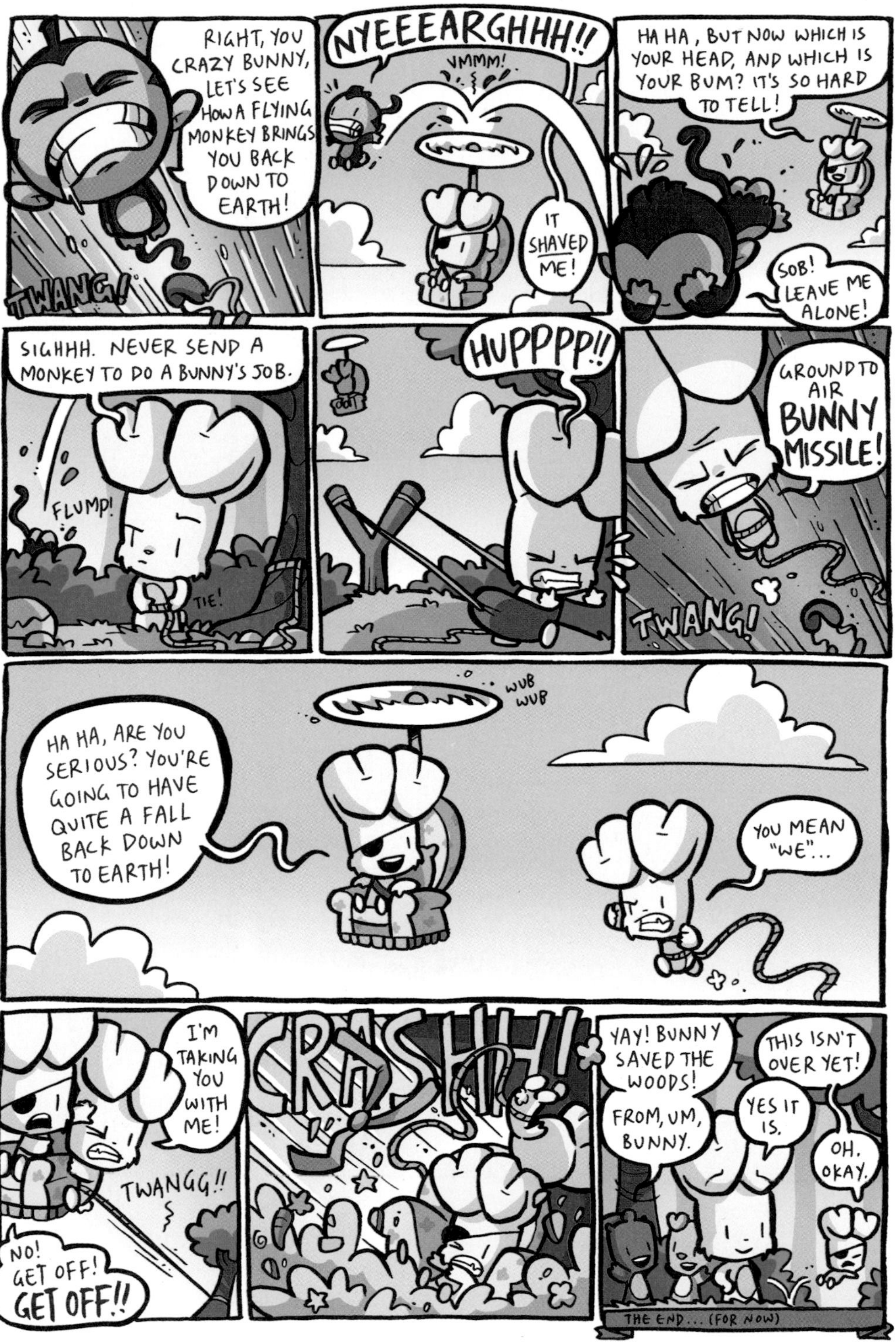
RIGHT, YOU CRAZY BUNNY, LET'S SEE HOW A FLYING MONKEY BRINGS YOU BACK DOWN TO EARTH!
TWANG!
NYEEEARGHHH!!
VMMM!
IT SHAVED ME!
HA HA, BUT NOW WHICH IS YOUR HEAD, AND WHICH IS YOUR BUM? IT'S SO HARD TO TELL!
SOB! LEAVE ME ALONE!
SIGHHH. NEVER SEND A MONKEY TO DO A BUNNY'S JOB.
FLUMP!
TIE!
HUPPPP!!
GROUND TO AIR BUNNY MISSILE!
TWANG!
WUB WUB
HA HA, ARE YOU SERIOUS? YOU'RE GOING TO HAVE QUITE A FALL BACK DOWN TO EARTH!
YOU MEAN "WE"...
I'M TAKING YOU WITH ME!
TWANGG!!
NO! GET OFF! GET OFF!!
CRASH!!
YAY! BUNNY SAVED THE WOODS!
FROM, UM, BUNNY.
THIS ISN'T OVER YET!
YES IT IS.
OH. OKAY.
THE END... (FOR NOW)

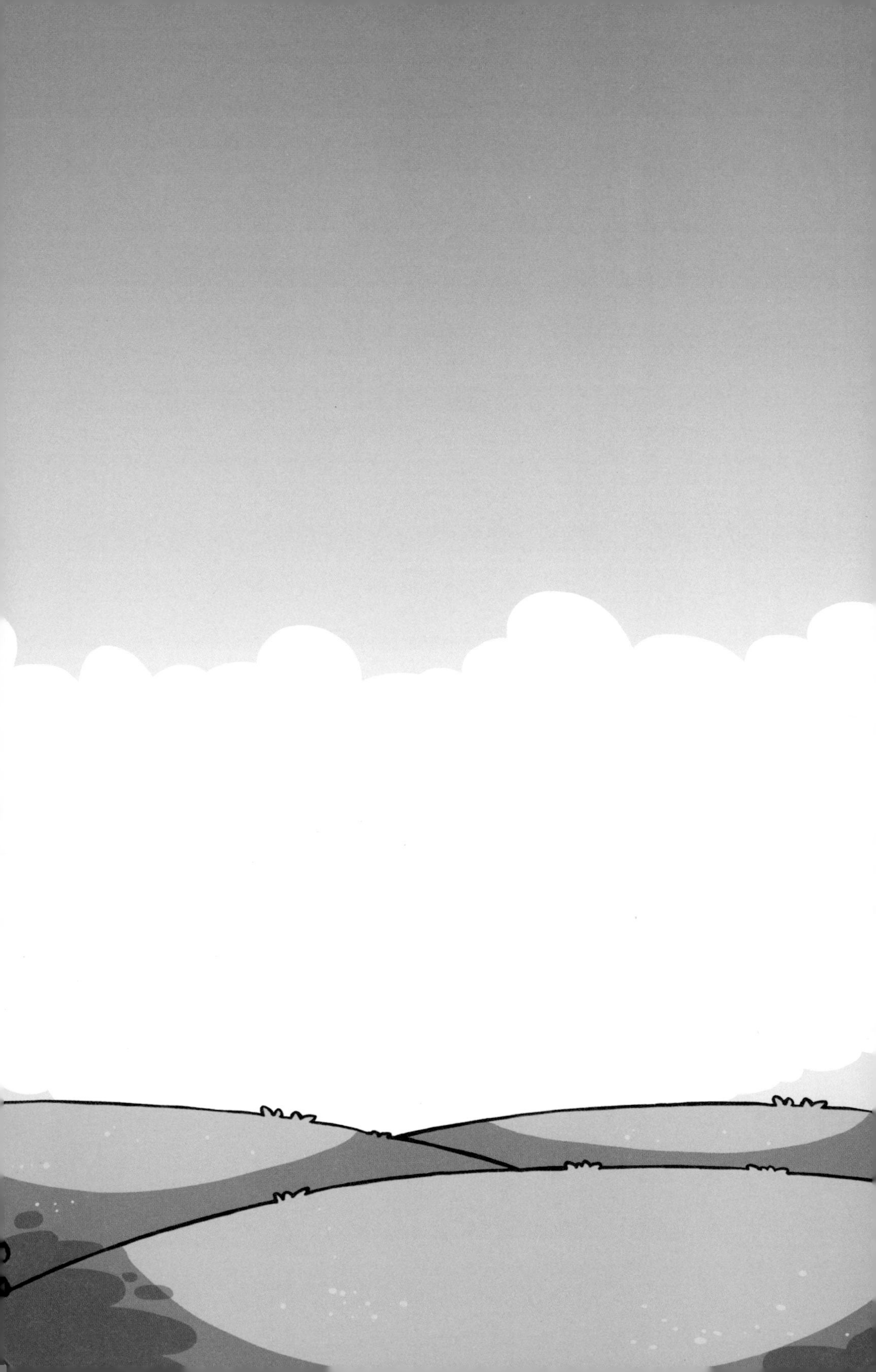

JAMIE SMART studied art, but it was just an excuse to practice drawing animals with googly eyes. He drew lots of comics and eventually started doing actual books. Jamie lives in Kent, England. You can visit him online at www.fumboo.com.

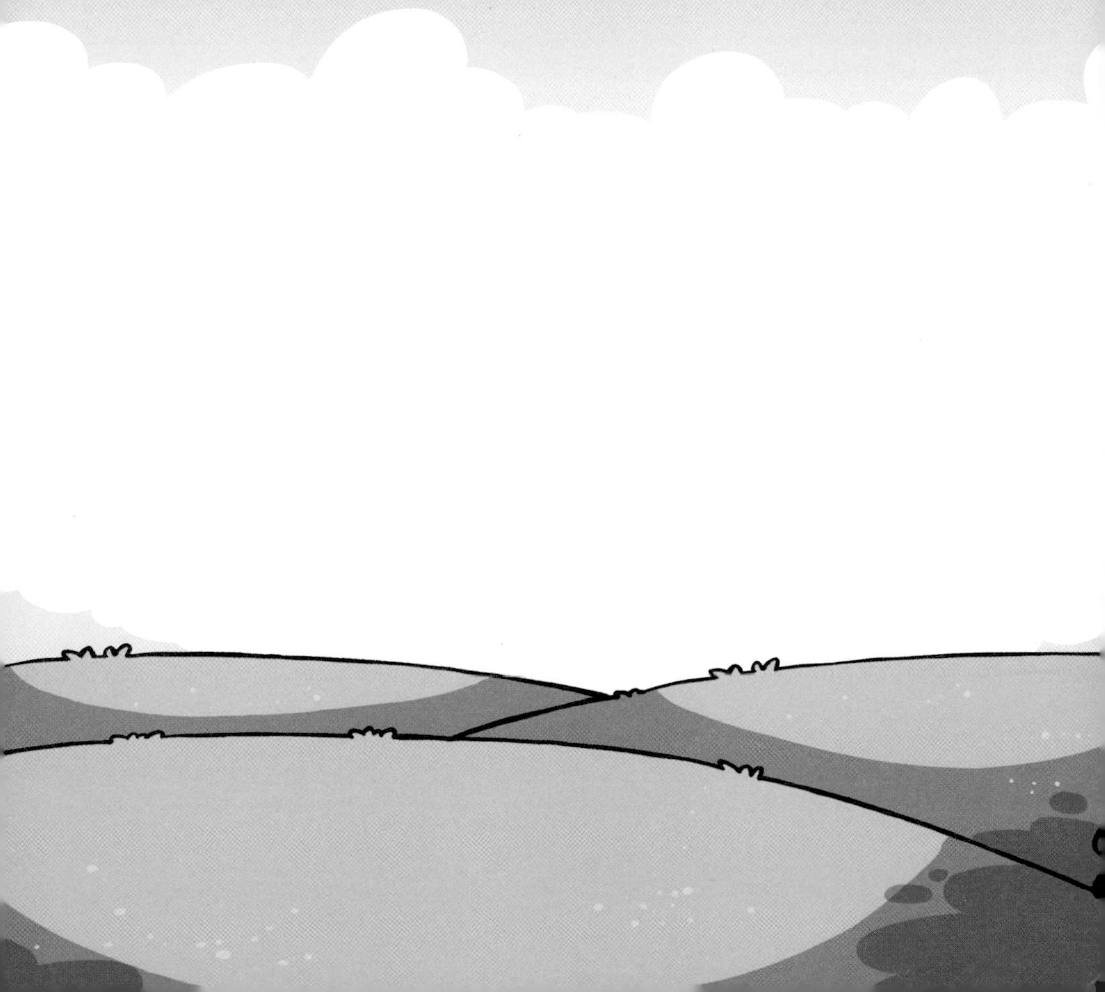

CHECK OUT THE HILARIOUS ADVENTURES OF BIRD & SQUIRREL BY JAMES BURKS!